The Legend of the Grey Man of Pawleys Island

Christine Vernon

Published by Christine Vernon, 2023.

This is a work of fiction. Similarities to real people, places, or events are entirely coincidental.

THE LEGEND OF THE GREY MAN OF PAWLEYS ISLAND

First edition. January 14, 2023.

Copyright © 2023 Christine Vernon.

ISBN: 979-8215643259

Written by Christine Vernon.

Table of Contents

PREFACE

I moved to Murrells Inlet, South Carolina in 2005, not having a single clue why I would choose this area to make my home. I had never heard of this small fishing village and had only been to Charleston, SC once many years prior. But something drew me here to its warm climate and pluff mud marshes. This tiny town is known as the Seafood Capital of South Carolina, a noticeably big title for such a small community. But it lives up to its name. It boasts of many fine restaurants and quaint little bars where salty ocean breezes blow.

Before I came here, I lived and studied in a farming community just outside Philadelphia, PA. I would learn how to grow my own food, take care of horses, chickens, and other livestock. But besides being a farm girl, I was also an artist. I studied charcoal, oil and acrylic painting and would sell my artwork as early as age 8. I always imagined having my own studio in the city or having multiple art shows at some of the finest galleries. But I would find myself moving from town to town never feeling quite like I fit in. Oh, I would have many friends and make a reasonable living, but something was missing. And it would not be until I reached the ripe old age of 40-something that God (or whom I call Spirit) would guide me to this little village and send me on a different path.

I met my second husband here in Murrells Inlet. A man who lived here approximately 40 years and had many friends who were some of the wittiest storytellers of the area. Mickey Spillane, Clarke Willcox to name a couple. Now each of these gentlemen could turn a phrase and tell a delightful story. One owned a famous home in our area, one that he and others say was haunted by a young plantation girl. The other man authored books about a brash detective. My husband gave me copies of their books, but my taste turned to Mr. Willcox's novels regarding the history and legends of our town. I inhaled each book. I memorized the tales and eventually turned to other authors and their writings. Next thing you know, I am hosting a ghost and history tour. Yes, I would become the next storyteller of the South Strand. I would have an insatiable appetite for historical documents and legendary tales. Eventually, I would be asked to lecture regarding our whimsical but dark past. Yes, I would learn not only about the heartbreaking tales of ghosts who had lost their loved ones and their lives, but also about true historical figures. The men and women who would give up their hopes, dreams and in the worst-case scenarios, their lives. Some, through no fault of their own, would come to this land by force. They were enslaved. Others were born and raised to deal with the hardships of living in a world fraught with dangers such as poisoness snakes and alligators hiding in the cypress swamps and grassy marshes.

I started to do research regarding the ancestors of our South Strand area and have written two other books regarding our local lore. My first was named The Old and New Legends of Murrells Inlet, South Carolina. This was a collection of short stories and legends such as a plantation ghost named Alice Flagg, Native American burial grounds, and other haunting stories. My second book, The Ghost of Alice, was a historical fiction story that dealt with the life of a young plantation girl who haunts a couple of locations in our marsh area. But there is one more well-known ghost story that is told especially during the hurricane season. This is the story of the Grey Man. Now, I know most people spell the word with an 'a' but to make sure there is no confusion with other books or stories, I have chosen to use 'e.'

I have been studying this legend of a man who dies tragically without ever knowing true love. It would evade him for much of his life. Some versions of the story claim he was quite young when he passed away. Others say he was middle-aged. I have even heard tell that it could be the ghost of a Spanish monk who walked these shores in 1526. We did have a brief time span when the Spanish came to settle our coastline but met with the inhospitable local native tribes. They were not welcomed, and war would ensue. Some natives were killed in battle, some enslaved. But I do not believe it is a monk that walks the shore, because the story told most suggests the first sighting of the Grey Man was in 1822 and many propose he was wearing a grey uniform or jacket. I have heard many versions of this story over the years. And therefore, I have chosen to write this rendition. I have done a lot of research and I found a few individuals who fit the description and period. I do not claim I have 100% knowledge that the characters are truly the Grey Man and his lost love. But with everything I have read, and the similarities in the towns they were both raised in, churches they attended, the friends they associated with, and previous storytellers of the past commenting on a gentleman with the same last name, I believe these particular people I write about are the most likely suspects.

This is a historical fiction novel which simply means that I have chosen characters from our distant past and I have creatively reconstructed what their days may have been like when they walked this Earth. The Colonial Period of South Carolina was a dangerous and politically confusing time for all. We were amid the birth of a new nation. Between fighting the local Native Americans for what was rightfully their land and pulling away from Great Britain, the colonial men and women were met with many challenges. Family ties were stretched to their limits, but it would be love that kept these brave individuals going. Love of family and country. When I started to do research for this novel, I had no idea it would propel me back to a place and time I only read about in history books. My first thought of authoring this novel was to tell a particularly good ghost story. It would take me into a genre I did not think I would write about...romance. This story is more about romance than paranormal, more about love than bloodshed. So, this so called 'ghost story' is more about lost love than lost souls.

We are about to go back to Revolutionary War days in one of the oldest cities in America- Charles Town, South Carolina. Now called Charleston, this town is steeped in old world mysteries. But I will also take you on a trip to my little village of Murrells Inlet and set the stage for plantation life in the Old South and the difficulties of its people, indigenous, enslaved and the Europeans that settled here. I do not claim to be a historian. On the contrary, I just write from my heart and what information I have gathered over the years falls into place.

Chapter One

It was an incredibly humid night in August of 1757 when a baby girl was born to John and Elizabeth Moore of Charles Town (later named Charleston), South Carolina. At 20 years of age this is Elizabeth's second child, having given birth to another baby girl in 1755. Her first girl was a difficult pregnancy. The child was very small and fragile but continued to thrive. Her house slave Chloe, a petite but muscular woman, remembered how anxious the family was regarding the frailness of the first child and stayed by Elizabeth's side throughout the night applying cold cloths to her forehead. She offered her mistress a small branch to bite down on. Chloe had seen her own mother use this when she was a midwife to the other slaves. She thought it was used to keep the pain down. Often a period of melancholy follows the woman after giving birth and Chloe also believed the stick would block evil from entering the mother's body.

But Elizabeth refused Cloe's offer and cried out from the pain as loud as she could. By early morning, her daughter would be brought into this world. There was much relief to both ladies when they heard the baby girl cry. She was a healthy one. Chloe took the newborn and washed her gently in a blue and white ceramic washbowl, then wrapped her tiny body in a small cream-colored blanket. She offered the child to Elizabeth and suddenly tears began to flow from her chestnut-colored eyes. Elizabeth already had a two-year-old to care for and she was already feeling overwhelmed. But she knew she would receive help from her family. Her husband's family and her own were quite wealthy and lived close by. Through the years, Elizabeth would dote on her children and fulfill all their needs. She would be their teacher and guardian. There were no schools for girls close by, but Elizabeth would teach her little girls everything from cooking, sewing, music and art. It was rare for little girls to have a formal education so Elizabeth would teach them what she could, just like her mother did for her.

John, a man of good stature and always well dressed, looked unkept due to having paced the floor all night in anticipation of finding out the gender of his child. Of course, a son would suit him fine, but he did have a sweet spot if it happened to be a girl. Once he heard the cries from the bedroom, he finally took a seat and breathed a heavy sigh. Chloe poked her head out of the bedroom door and smiled at her master and in her heavy Gullah accent told him, "Yessum it be a helty baby girl." John immediately rose and pushed the bedroom door open. He started to approach Elizabeth but stopped just a few feet away. She was covered in sweat but had joy in her eyes. He stepped softly to her side, placed his hand upon her brow and wiped her light chestnut brown hair from her face. He was unable to speak. All smiled down at his bride and listened to the whimpers of his baby girl. It would be days before they could think of a name for her. They both wished for a boy but had not thought of a girl's name. So, after some negotiating, they named their new baby girl after John's mother, Rachel.

The Charles Town home would be full of family and friends for the next couple of weeks. There would be much celebration at the announcement of Elizabeth's and John's second child. Their first baby girl was named Eliza, but it would be easier for all to call her Lizzy. The family was quite liked and had a good reputation in Charles Town. They were also quite respected and once Elizabeth was well enough, the family of four would be seen at their local church, St. Philips. Although they lived in St. Thomas Parish, which was 9 miles outside of Charles Town, Elizabeth's family, the Vanderhorst's were instrumental in helping the church rebuild after a terrible fire destroyed the original wooden building. After the fire, the families felt it was safer to build their own family homes with red brick.

Life for a young mother in the colonial Charles Town settlement was still quite a struggle. It was required of the wives and mothers to keep house, cook (unless they were fortunate to have a house servant), sew and doctor anyone who was sick. But the most critical position of the wife was to be a good mother. Her role according to her husband and the church was to increase the population with God-fearing children who could bring prosperity to this fledgling village. In 1757, the town had a dozen or so streets, but the population was growing with every passing day.

The family owned quite a few acres northwest of the city so there was no concern regarding lack of food. John Moore was not just a planter by trade. Although his plantation was plentiful with fertile soil near the Cooper River which was perfect for planting rice, sweet potatoes, and corn, he was also a merchant. In just a few years, John Moore was to become the local representative of St. Thomas and St Dennis Parish as well as a local justice. As a local justice this meant he and other Charlestonians must keep the peace. He would have his hands full. Especially during these times of expansion into the West. There was still the threat of attack by local natives. Rachel was born during the French and Indian War. Although much of the fighting was going on in the Ohio Valley, this led to uprisings as far south as Georgia. Local tribes such as the Cherokee, Waccamaw, Catawba and others who had traded with the Europeans were now questioning the treaties that were signed between them. They were being evicted from their homeland and this was not acceptable.

Not long after Rachel's birth, there was an attack on a local family who settled further west of Charles Town. The mother was found just outside the city limits. She recounted to the justices, including Rachel's father John Moore, that she and her husband were visited by the local tribe. They were upset with the increase of Europeans on their tribal land. They had been forced off the land that was promised to them through treaties signed by her husband and other officials. She said her husband spoke to them until almost dawn. When she and her husband went to bed, the natives entered the home and killed her husband. They struck her with an axe, but she played dead until they left. It took an entire day for her to make her way by horse to Charles Town. After she told the committee of justices what she knew, she collapsed and was taken to a local doctor.

Local slaves took note of the upheaval. The plantation owners were concerned that their servants had ideas of their own to rebel. The population of South Carolina was 50/50...50% white, 50% black/indentured servants. If the enslaved ever had the opportunity to unify a plan of attack, they could take over much of the smaller settlements, gain control of any weapons and then turn their attention to Charles Town. This would be the end of plantation life in the South. Without the free labor of slaves, farms and large plantations would have to hire workers or owners and their families would have to endure the back breaking work of planting and harvesting. And England would not like to lose their investment in this New World. The riches provided by plantations as well as the taxes on goods grown in America had made His Majesty the King of England incredibly happy.

Elizabeth knew that emotions were running high. It was up to her to keep her daughter safe from harm of all kinds. There was still the memory of the first yellow fever epidemic that struck Charles Town in 1699, killing about 15% of the population. Many of them were children. The disease would bring a yellow hue to the infected person. If you lived through the sickness, you could become immune. But, for children and newcomers to the port city, it was devastating. Symptoms such as fever, exhaustion, delirium, and vomiting would be exhibited. Yellow fever continued to strike the coastal area at least 5 more times in the early 1700s. It was highly contagious and spread quickly from house to house. Many had to be quarantined so local businesses and shops had to close. Everything came to a stop. Cargo ships heard the news of the outbreak and would go to a different harbor to avoid the plague. There was a lack of medicine and panic would set in. Then a terrible outbreak of influenza hit the town, taking another 15% of the residents. Very few made it through that illness. Elizabeth herself had lost family during that period. Everyone she knew did.

But happier times were coming with this tiny little bundle and Elizabeth could not be more pleased. But on occasion, there would be a moment when she would tighten her grip on Rachel. When family and friends would visit the small family, Elizabeth would always stay within earshot of her baby. The family thought she was being overprotective of her daughters. But Elizabeth thought it was normal for a mother to always keep a keen eye on her children.

But as for John, he was responsible for keeping his family together. He would work long hours overseeing his small plantation. He was also a very savvy merchant. He bought and traded items and livestock daily to increase his wealth. He owned quite a few horses and he had to keep a constant eye on them. It seemed one day two of his marsh tacky horses walked off the farm. This seemed very unusual especially since the gate was closed and locked when they went missing. John knew he was a target for newcomers in the area. When there was no sign of his horses, he placed an advertisement in the local newspaper offering a reward for their safe return. Horse thieves were common in this parish.

A few weeks after Rachel's birth Elizabeth received a visit from her brother and sister-in law, the Neufvilles. Her husband's sister, also named Elizabeth, and her husband who was named Jonathan, were extremely excited about the new baby in the family. It became very confusing with the similarities of their names, which met with laughter on many an occasion. So, to not cause any more problems, the family would call John's sister Betsy, and her husband by his full name, Jonathan. They were also expecting their own bundle of joy in just a few months' time. The husbands were thrilled to know that both the woman would help each other raise their children. Betsy had already given birth to a little boy the year before, Jonathon Jr. She had hoped for her second child to be a girl. But Betsy had a more challenging time with her first birth. He was a breech birth; the family was not sure if the baby and mother would survive. But Betsy was a strong and determined lady no matter what the circumstances and she recovered quickly. Betsy would get her way. She always did. Even her husband Jonathan had a challenging time saying no to his wife. She was not one to back down. Even at five foot 2 inches tall she was a force to reckon with. This was quite unusual for ladies of this time. The majority of woman were quite calm and reserved. Being emotional or outspoken was not a characteristic that men found interesting in a mate. But Betsy was one to keep her family and friends on their toes. She refused to let men tell her what her place was in society. Normally a woman expecting a baby would spend her pregnancy at home and not march through the streets of the city. But not Betsy. She was determined to see Elizabeth and Rachel, her newborn niece.

In her usual style, Betsy raps on the porch door and nudges it open. She did not like to wait for anyone to answer knowing Elizabeth had her hands full with two children. Chloe ran towards the Neufvilles, bowed her head, and apologized for not getting there faster.

"No need," says Betsy, "Please inform my sister-in-law that we have arrived."

Chloe nods and takes Betsy's wrap along with Jonathan's cape and hat. She rushes upstairs to fetch her master and tell her mistress that company was in the house.

Elizabeth smiled at Chloe before she even got a word out of her mouth.

"Yes, Chloe, I heard my beloved Mrs. Neufville announce her presence. Just inform Mr. Moore that his brother and his wife have arrived."

"You do not have to tell me either, Chloe" says John as he walks across the hall towards his wife's bedroom. "My lovely sister-in-law has made her presence known to every personage east of the Cooper River."

Chloe felt as though she was being pulled in many directions. She nodded her head once more and whispered her usual 'yessum' to Mr. and Mrs. Moore.

Chloe ran back down the stairs to tell the Neufvilles that her master and mistress will be down shortly. But before she can utter a sound Betsy begins to question Chloe.

"And how is your mistress? Are there any issues to which I may render my services? And where is the newborn? And Lizzy, why has she not greeted her aunt and uncle?"

Chloe cannot get a word out of her mouth. She does not know where to start first.

"My gracious Sister, it should be I to answer your curious questions instead of Chloe. Let us join in the parlor and I will be happy to keep you abreast of the current situation." Everyone looked upwards and saw Elizabeth walking down the staircase with her husband John.

"Of course, sister dear. You may tell me all about your current situation and how I may be of service to you."

As the ladies entered the parlor both men greeted, shook hands, and knew they would not be able to get a word into the conversation. John reached for the brandy and both men headed out the door to catch up on news of the port city. There was much to discuss regarding a possible uprising from the slaves.

Chloe knew that the ladies would want tea and headed towards the back of the house to heat the water. She would have to hurry so she could get back upstairs to take care of Lizzy and Rachel. Her position had become more justified. She will be needed increasingly more but in time will need an extra hand.

Chapter Two

A few months later after the birth of Rachel, Betsy would have a healthy baby boy just before Christmas of 1757. They decided to name the child William but would fondly nickname him 'Will'. This time Betsy would have no problem with her pregnancy and in her usual strong-willed way was up and running the household in no time.

Both Elizabeth and Betsy lived in 2 story homes made of red brick. They were almost the same in every aspect. Both homes were narrow but sufficient for such generous size families. At least so far. The ladies had mentioned to their husbands that space had become a bit confined for their growing families and their needs. Of course, John and his brother-in-law begged to differ. They felt for now the homes would suffice. Many families were moving into Charles Town and new homes were being constructed throughout the port city which caused Betsy to feel a bit claustrophobic. She enjoyed spending many of her days with Elizabeth further outside the walls of Charles Town. John and Elizabeth had a sizable number of acres and room to expand if necessary.

But John was more concerned with his newly formed company and expanding his business. John spent most of his time in the city. He was particularly good at bartering and was known to make honest deals with other farmers. John Moore would become a man people could rely on if they needed anything. But John had become more disenchanted with the regulations set down by England. Many merchants were speaking out against the unfair taxes on tea and stamps. The taxes were set to cover the cost of the French Indian War. The merchants and farmers felt they were being used to fund a war they were not directly involved in. Most of the fighting was further north in an area named Ohio. The French lay claim to this land, but Britain would eventually take it over, and this would cost both money and lives. And Charles

Town was a growing, wealthy port city and taxes would begin to climb steadily.

Betsy and her husband felt uneasy regarding the war. The Neufvilles were French Huguenots. Jonathan's family ancestors were forced out of France due to persecution. The Protestants refused to renounce their faith and join the Catholic Church under King Louis XIV. Troops were dispatched through the countryside to hunt down the heretics. Many would lose everything; land, liberty, and lives. Both John and Johnathan spent many hours speaking with their neighbors regarding the politics of the day. The local merchants had begun to make plans of their own if Britain were to tax them any further.

Both Betsy and Elizabeth had other matters to take care of. They would spend many hours together at each other's homes. The ladies felt it was much easier to have their children raised together. Family was extremely important in these early settlement days. Will and Rachel spent every moment of the day together. Both were fed together, took their daily afternoon naps together, even dressed in similar clothes. People would often ask if they were twin girls. Children of the time were dressed in long gowns and dresses, including the males until they were able to walk. Betsy would become a little defensive when people assumed Will was a girl and immediately began to dress Will in blue outfits. Elizabeth and Betsy would lay the children down for naps each afternoon after supper. When the ladies would check on the children while they napped, they would find them holding onto each other in a sweet embrace. But once the Neufville family returned to their home, Elizabeth would notice that Rachel would become fussy when it was her bedtime. She rolled to her side and looked for Will to be there. Betsy noticed the same with Will when night fell. It took hours for the boy to finally fall asleep. But, when the ladies visited again, the children would nap together without any fuss.

As the children grew older, the women would continue to add to their families. Betsy would have another boy named Peter in 1764.

Isaac soon after. Finally, Betsy would give birth to a daughter of her own years later. A pleasant change after raising a series of loud, rough housing boys.

Elizabeth would have many girls and only one boy...just the opposite of Betsy. Betsy's household would be a whirlwind of male energy while Elizabeth's country home would be a bit quieter. Having large families together for holidays or events would take a great deal of planning, something John and Jonathan wished to avoid. There was much to do to keep all these mouths fed. It became inevitable for the men to buy more servants to help with both households and the fieldwork. Chloe could use a hand managing the children. They were certainly a handful and Elizabeth was growing more exhausted with each passing day. Although she grew up in a large family of siblings herself, she had a challenging time getting her own brood ready for the day. Betsy was in the same predicament. Her mischievous children were full of pranks and often did not commence with their schoolwork.

But not Will. Will was a quiet and obedient child, quite the opposite of his brothers. He looked just like his father, tall, thin with the same steel grayish blue eyes. He seemed thirsty for knowledge, especially regarding medicine. He was always around the animals in the field and administering help to them if they were injured. Once a small bird flew into the parlor window of his house. The thump made everyone in the home jump. Will's mother rose from her needlework and discovered the poor creature unable to move. Will immediately took the small bird from his mother's hands. Betsy knelt next to her son. "Will, what are you proposing to do with the creature? Unfortunately, I feel its time has come."

Will cradled the bird. "It is only in shock...frozen with fear. I will nurse it. It may stand a chance."

Betsy was taken with her son's empathy for the little wren. She felt in her heart that he would grow to be a very compassionate fellow. And hopefully, a fine doctor. She watched as Will carefully walked towards the small barn behind their property as he carried his precious patient. Betsy could only smile and go back to her needlepoint.

As Will grew older he and Rachel became closer. She had taken an interest in everything Will learned in his schooling. Rachel was not satisfied with just learning how to sew a hem on a dress or how to properly serve tea. On the contrary, she wanted to learn everything her male counterparts were taught. But there is one thing she does enjoy the most, her music. At the early age of 7 she accomplished playing a short piece on the family piano. Elizabeth was quite proud of her little prodigy and was happy to continue her lessons. Whenever Rachel would play piano, Will would stand outside the window of the music room quietly so Rachel would not hear him. He would smile to himself whenever he heard her hit a wrong note. But she would practice over and over until she conquered the piece. He knew she was not one to quit and he admired that in his cousin. Occasionally, his brothers would catch him by the window and make fun of him. Will found them quite annoying. Always running and causing commotion. But Will had better things to do. For instance, he hoped Rachel and the family would come and stay in Charles Town during the summer months. Sometimes, life by the river would be incredibly uncomfortable due to the mosquitoes. No one was comfortable during that season. Many moved to their summer homes in Charles Town. Others to beach homes along the shore or to the north near the mountains. Unfortunately, the slaves would be the worst off having to endure the humidity and many diseases.

Over time both John Moore's family would grow and prosper. The children were entering their teen years and John decided to purchase another slave to help him with deliveries and goods for his growing mercantile business. The servant's name was Abraham and he had worked on another plantation that had met with hard times. His master had to separate and sell the family of slaves he owned and John saw promise in Abraham. He was 5 foot 8 inches tall and had a sound build. John noticed that Abraham only owned one set of clothes, his blue woolen pants, and a torn cotton shirt. He would have to purchase clothing for the man if he were to be working at his business in the city.

As John talked to the plantation owner regarding purchasing him, Abraham could only think of what his family was going through. He was devastated with news his family were to be torn apart. His wife, Maryann, had already been sold to a gentleman from the Allston family and was sent further north. Elizabeth hoped John could acquire Maryann as another house servant, but John could not afford both. The most devastating event was the loss of Abraham's and Maryann's daughter Cubby. She would have to stay with her current mistress and master. Not yet in her teens, she would be at the will of other men on the plantation. Abraham and his wife knew this and could only pray that their little girl would not be scarred emotionally by these circumstances. The decision by their master to break up the family had been made swiftly and no one was able to say goodbye. This family of three were to be ripped apart. And so were their hearts.

John told Abraham to climb aboard his carriage and both men headed back towards John's home. Abraham would be introduced to his new work environment to oversee the horses and take provisions to and from the dock off the Cooper River to John's mercantile store. John had heard good things about Abraham from his previous master and hoped what he heard was the truth. Abraham was bright and knew how to count and add numbers quickly. That would be an asset to John and his business. In time, the two men would work well together, but John could see the sadness in his servant's eyes. John would ask Abraham about his wife Maryann, but Abraham could not speak. It was too painful for him to talk about her. There was still hatred in his heart regarding their circumstances. But Abraham would hide his anger. He wanted the Moore family to believe that all was well. That he was resigned to his fate. But Abraham would not reveal his true intentions. He had made a vow between him and God. Somehow, he would find his way back to his wife and daughter. Every night, he vowed to God that he would find a way to bring his family together and leave the South and head north. But the timing had to be perfect. How would he perform such a plan? All he knew was the last name of the man who bought his wife and heard she was further north of Charles Town. Abraham hoped that Cubby was still with his former master so he may come back for her. He prayed for a plan. Night and day, he prayed for salvation.

Abraham always kept his ears open for any information regarding his family. He would listen to customer's conversations at John's store praying that someone may mention her name. On one particular day he heard from a customer the name 'Allston' mentioned and an area called 'Murray's Inlet.' The client was remarking to John Moore that this little-known area was becoming exceedingly popular and many families from the Charles Town area were expanding their holdings to that coastal village. The coastal marsh region would later be named after one of the area's wealthiest plantation owners, J. Murrell. There were many new plantations springing up along the Waccamaw River and more slaves were being sent to that region for indigo and rice production. Abraham repeated the words Murray's Inlet and Allston over and over again so he would not forget. He prayed that if he ever escaped, he would find Maryann there in this new coastal town and take her and their daughter north. But tears entered his eyes as he thought about his poor wife having to endure field work in a location that was still wilderness. Having to clear the land of trees and brush near any river was fraught with dangers such as poisoness snakes and alligators. He knew too many of his own had been maimed and killed by these creatures. Raising rice and indigo was tedious and dangerous work.

Indigo had been introduced to the South from a Charles Town family named Lucas. A young woman named Eliza who would bring this plant from the West Indies and create an American Empire within the British Empire. The river system and the Carolina climate were perfect for the indigo plant. It was valued highly by European countries. It would give the colonists a taste of wealth they had not seen before, and Britain watched carefully as the colonists became botanical experts of this new world. Most everyone in Charles Town knew Eliza Lucas and her family. She was a major source of information when it came to growing and harvesting indigo, but it was the enslaved that did the backbreaking work. Many came from regions of the West Indies and African coast where rice and indigo were prized. Between 1745 until 1775 the Indigo Bonanza made everyone in the county wealthy. Even John and Elizabeth had just started this intricate process of planting, harvesting, and extracting the beautiful blue dye from the plants.

As John's business increased, he was able to purchase more servants. But there was one person he felt should be added to his clan of workers. It had always pulled on his heart how much Abraham had missed his family. Normally this would not be an issue of concern to him. However, Abraham was a hard worker. A dedicated man. John would see him work tirelessly until he collapsed. But there was always sadness in his eyes. And he knew why. He imagined how he would have felt to be ripped away from his family. So, John made it his mission to acquire Abraham's daughter, Cubby, and bring her to their household. It was unclear exactly where his wife Maryann was sent, but he was sure he could find Cubby.

John not only wanted to acquire Cubby for Abraham but also felt it was time for Rachel to have someone close to her age to help her and her sisters. This whole scheme would work out well for all, especially his wife, Elizabeth. She worked harder than any woman he knew, and it was time for the family to expand both their property, his business, and their holdings. Cubby could help with all this.

Chapter Three

Life in Charles Town was growing more exciting each day in the 1770s. The U.S. Customs House was being built for the city. A huge Greek Revival structure with massive white columns overlooked both the city and harbor. The city was bustling with Protestants settlers from Ireland. Many were encouraged to leave their home country and settle in the New World, full of promise. Thousands came and worked tirelessly for the plantation owners. Others were given land and began their own settlements. The port city grew at an incredible rate.

Both the Moore and Neufville families were encouraged by the thousands of refugees flooding the city. John's businesses had grown, and he worked late hours to keep up with demand for construction materials needed for housing.

Jonathon Neufville was quite busy himself. He worked for St. Phillips and St. Michael's Parish. He had looked for a position at the Exchange and Provost Building. It was a huge undertaking and would be the site of a customs house, market, meeting place as well as a military prison. It was a large 2 story Georgian design. The city had moved up in culture and style and both Elizabeth and Betsy were excited about how modern their town had become. They were particularly excited about all the new styles and fashions coming from Europe. Elizabeth would sneak by her husband's store and take the first pick of any fabric or ribbons that arrived by boat. And, of course, Betsy would be the first to find out about the newest patterns and silks.

Once Elizabeth returned with her arms full of yards of the newest cloth, she would run to her sewing room and begin the task of sewing. She loved to sew and create beautiful dresses and gowns. On this day she worked on a particular gown for a grand occasion... the wedding of her daughter Lizzy. The house was a frenzy of activity. Servants polished silver and cooked a small feast in the kitchen.

Everyone was involved with preparations except Rachel. She sat and dreamt of her own wedding day. She hoped one day to be wed and start a family of her own. But today was for Lizzy. Rachel was honestly happy for her sister, but she could only think of herself and her future. She was at an age where her mind wandered as she gazed out the music room window. She reached her teenage years, and she had grown into a fine young lady. No more braids or pigtails. The few freckles she was born with still had their place on her nose but had slightly faded with age. She looked more like her mother every day. Her chestnut-brown eyes had a shimmer to them, and her mahogany brown hair flowed down her back in ringlets.

She may be petite, but she would prove to be a quest for any man. She loved to ask questions regarding the politics of the times and was always ready for a debate. Her mother would roll her eyes and shake her finger whenever she felt Rachel had gone too far. She was told to 'respect her elders' and 'a young lady should listen and learn from others who have lived to a mature age.'

But one other question entered her mind. Who was she to marry? She had heard her parents bring up this subject before behind closed doors. They had looked for a suitable husband for Rachel, but she never knew who they referred to. Her older sister Lizzy had gained the affection of one of the Allston's from the Murrells Inlet area. They were a remarkably successful family who two plantations. They were the second richest family behind the Wards who owned three plantations and nearly 200 slaves. Lizzy was 16 and her parents were prepared to announce the engagement by throwing a party for the couple. But Rachel did not care much for this young man. She did not understand what attracted Lizzy to Mr. Allston? He was at least twenty years her senior with a bit of a heavy waistline and his hair was thinning. He had made an advance towards Rachel, too. In fact, many of them. He would give her a quick glance and an upturned smile behind her sister's back. He immediately rushed to Rachel when she entered a room and held a chair for her. Once he had the gall to hold her hand and ask if they may speak in private. She swept his advances away with an upturned nose and told Mr. Billy Allston to hush and not speak such words to her. But Rachel did not have the heart to tell her sister what an utter cad she thought Billy was. She knew Lizzy would not believe her. She was desperately in love with him. So, Rachel held her tongue and hoped love would bloom between the two of them. And hoped Billy would prove to be an exceptional husband.

There was someone else who noticed Billy Allston's affection towards Rachel. It was Will. He did not like the way Billy looked at Rachel. Rachel had also mentioned to Will how she felt uncomfortable around Billy. Will felt threatened by Billy's advances towards Rachel and became more jealous each time Billy's name was mentioned. Jealousy was a new emotion for him. He was always protective of Rachel, but jealous? Or was this feeling of jealousy really love? He had always loved Rachel and would do anything for her. In all the years they were raised together they always looked upon their relationship as one of brother and sister. But now that Billy Allston had come into view, his feelings had grown deeper for his cousin. Cousin. He had to continue to remind himself of that word. They were cousins after all. But he knew of other cousins who married in other families. It would not be so different...would it? He had one way to find out. He would ask Rachel for her hand in marriage.

It was Saturday and the family were getting ready to announce their engagement. Hearing this news, Will rode to Rachel's home and waited for her to finish her lessons that fall afternoon. He peered over the ledge of the window and could see Rachel with her sister Lizzy. The two girls embraced and smiled. Will could not hear what was said, but knew it had to be about the engagement. Rachel turned to leave the music room when she heard a tap on the window. She smiled and chuckled when she saw it was Will and immediately ran to open the window.

"I take it you have heard the good news of Lizzy and Mr. Allston? It will be announced at dinner. I do hope you will arrive in time tonight?"

Will looks to see if anyone is still in the room. "Rachel, may I speak with you in private? Let us walk by the river."

Rachel shook her head yes and proceeded to the front door. Will met her at the bottom step and took her by the arm. They walked towards the water; the sun sparkled off the gentle waves. Once they were by the riverbank away from her home, Will turned to Rachel and took a deep breath.

"Rachel, we have known each other a lifetime. There has never been a day when we have lost each other's friendship or trust. I am forever yours."

Rachel is a little confused by his words and replies, "Of course we shall be together forever. We are each other's confidantes. There is nothing I would not do for you. You have always been my ally and I shall forever love you, dear cousin."

Will places his hand around her waist and presses Rachel a little closer. "Yes, my Rachel. I will always love you. And it is here and now I ask the question."

He paused briefly and took a deep breath. "Be my wife, dearest Rachel."

Rachel pulled away from his embrace. She twirled around and lost her footing. She stumbled to the ground but managed to regain her balance. Will reached for her and helped her to her feet. But this time he pulled her closer. Closer than she has ever been to him. She did not say a word. All she could do was look into his steel blue grey eyes. She was powerless to move. She knew she should walk away. But part of her did not want to. She held her breath, wondering what his next move would be.

Then a voice was heard from the distance. Lizzy was calling out for Rachel. Rachel quickly looked toward the house and answered her sister back. Will only has this moment to convince Rachel that he was true to his word. He placed his finger under her chin and brought her gaze back to his. He slowly leaned in towards her and kissed her. Gently at first, but as she pulled away, he pressed tighter. She had never been kissed before. Rachel found herself at his will. She slowly raised her arms around his neck. It suddenly became clear that she did love her cousin more than she thought. Rachel heard her sister call her name again. Rachel dropped her arms and pushed Will away. She could not say a word and ran back towards the house.

Lizzy spotted Rachel rushing back from the riverside. She was flushed and breathed heavily. Lizzy smiled and giggled at her sister.

"Dear sister, you did not have to wind yourself. It was not that urgent a call. Mother hoped you would help her prepare the seating chart for tonight."

Rachel composed herself and brushed back her matted hair. She took a deep breath and followed Lizzy toward the dining room. But before she closed the front door, she took one last look out towards the river. Will had gone. Taking another deep breath, she slowly walked in. She must compose herself before her mother saw her and before the guests arrived.

The engagement party began at three o'clock and carriages arrived at a steady pace. Relatives and close friends were invited to the event. But one soul did not appear...Will. Rachel was quite anxious to see if Will would arrive. What would he say or do? She could not deal with this situation with a house full of guests. She would have to put on a stellar performance for everyone. It would be an arduous task, however. Everyone repeatedly asked Rachel if she knew if Will would arrive. Even Billy Allston asked her when he would appear. Rachel had a feeling Billy knew Will was displeased with him. Billy was amused whenever he approached Rachel at functions and noticed the uncomfortable reaction from Will. Rachel could only shrug her shoulders and make an excuse why Will had not surfaced. She had presumed he was delayed taking care of another injured creature.

Everyone knew Will was contemplating medical school and they accepted her answer. But Rachel knew better. And she grew more anxious as the night wore on.

In the late hours of the evening, the guests withdrew. Carriages rolled away with a syncopated rhythm of horse's hooves until the last was just out of earshot. Rachel hoped that Will was not cross with her for not answering his proposal. How could she? It was neither the time nor place. And what would her family think?

Rachel did not sleep that night. She was extremely restless and knew she would have to speak with Will the following day. She would have to give him an answer. But even she did not know what that answer was. Not yet.

The morning light broke through Rachel's window and told her it was time to get prepared for the day. She would not eat or drink but would rush out the door towards the barn. She spotted Abraham as he tended to the horses and asked that he prepare a carriage for her. Rachel was not to go to town without an escort and asked if he would make the trip with her. He would have to seek permission from her father first. This was a bit troubling. She would have to make an excuse for the journey to Charles Town. She fashioned a story of wanting to find a wedding gift for her sister. When John heard her story, he permitted Abraham to go, but asked that he come back as soon as possible.

The trip to town was only a short distance and Abraham was glad to be away from the dock. He noticed that Rachel was preoccupied in thought. He began to make small talk regarding the weather and asked how Miss Lizzy was during this happy time.

Rachel turned to Abraham and asked, "Abraham, if you were in love with someone but you were afraid your family would be against the union, would you still marry, or would you be obliged to serve your parents and break the heart of that one person who truly loved you?"

Abraham was quite taken aback by this rather long and complicated question. He had an idea what she had asked and could only answer one way.

"Miss Rachel, I only knows one ting…Love. It why we here. To love, be love, dats all." Abraham thought of his wife Maryann and how he and she had loved each other from the first time they met on the plantation 15 years ago. He and she did not have the proper type of wedding that settlers had but it was still a marriage for them, nonetheless. It would be a union until the day they died. That was their promise to each other. And he meant to keep that promise.

Rachel gently nodded her head in agreement. She would speak with Will and together they would find a time and place to make their feelings known to the family. She turned and smiled at Abraham and was quiet the rest of the way.

The carriage wandered through the cobbled streets until it stopped at her aunt and uncle's home. She slowly approached the door and knocked. One of Aunt Betsy's servants opened the door and kindly let Rachel in. Before Rachel could ask to see Will, he came around the corner and stopped suddenly at the sight of his cousin. Neither said a word. Will was nervous about the reason for her visit. He could only utter the words 'good morning.'

Rachel smiled and ran to him holding her arms open waiting for an embrace. Will was thrilled at this response, picked up Rachel, and whirled her around. He suddenly realized that his family could walk in at any moment. He took Rachel by the hand and guided her into the parlor and closed the door behind them.

Will bent down to kiss her. Rachel quickly looked around to make sure no one was in the room. They had much to talk about and needed to do it quickly. They took a seat on a small bench and discussed their future. It would be a long and complicated issue, but Will was adamant he would marry Rachel. Rachel was quite nervous to approach their parents. Rachel was a little young to marry at only 15 years of age. And to bring up this subject when it was Lizzy's time to wed may be a little daunting to the parents. Will had prepared to leave Charles Town for school in Virginia and they needed to plan to marry before he left. They found they both genuinely loved each other. The matter would first be brought up to Rachel's parents. They decided to leave immediately for Rachel's home and ask for permission to marry.

Rachel headed back to the carriage and Abraham took the reins. Will ran to the carriage house to retrieve his horse and told them he would catch up with them soon. Rachel pleaded with Abraham to go as fast as he could. Abraham heard the urgency in her voice and grabbed his riding crop to hurry the team back home.

Both Elizabeth and John were home for the midday meal and had resigned to the parlor for tea. Will and Rachel met outside the stable of her home and held each other's hands. They proceeded through the front door straight into the parlor and asked if they could have a word with her parents. Her parents looked at each other, turned to Rachel, asked if there was a problem.

Rachel was tongue tied. She looked up at Will and would let him speak for them both. But once the words fell from Will's mouth for Rachel's hand there was a resounding 'NO' from both parents.

"Absolutely not," replied Elizabeth. "You are both children... and cousins. This matter is not to be brought up again." Her husband, John only sat and nodded in agreement with his wife. Will tried to address John again and pleaded for him to hear him out. John stood up from his seat and walked towards them both. He placed a hand on Will's shoulder and his other hand on his daughter's head. He loved them both. Will was like a son to him. But he had to put his foot down and end the conversation. The answer was no. There would be no more discussion.

Rachel and Will bowed their heads and walked slowly from the room. Once outside, Will turned to Rachel. It was not over yet. They may be able to defend themselves to his parents. Maybe they would listen to their side and agree with their plan. But John overheard their conversation. He told Rachel she must stay home and asked Will to leave. He hoped Will would not bring up the subject with his parents. John once again warned the two that this was a finished subject.

Will headed back to Charles Town. He did not heed John Moore's advice and hoped his parents would agree to their marriage. And if they agreed, they may convince Rachel's parents to let them wed. But once he met with his parents that night he was met with the same answer. Betsy was extremely troubled by Will's request. She was quite embarrassed to hear the children had gone to Elizabeth and John first. Their decision would not be swayed by Will's pleas. The matter was closed. But this would not stop how Will felt for Rachel. Maybe once he came back from medical school he would try again. But that would take some time. Years, in fact. Could they both wait that long? Neither one wanted to disobey their parents. But they also wanted to follow their hearts. They were meant to be together, forever.

The following day, Will rode back to Rachel. He would have to tell her the sad news about his parents' decision. How could they make their parents see that they were in love?

The two would spend the day together by the river. The autumn air was becoming cooler and soon the holidays would arrive. But once the holiday season was over, Will would have to go to Virginia to finish his education and then to medical school. Rachel had hoped he could change schools and stay in Charles Town, but his father was insistent that he go north.

In the following days, Will and Rachel spent as much time as they could together. It would be nearly impossible for their parents to keep them from seeing each other. They had always been together through everything. Laughter, tears, heartache. Whenever Rachel needed a friend for advice Will was quick to be at her side. When she fell while horseback riding and injured her leg, Will gave her comfort, and nursed her. The family never saw anything unusual about their companionship. They felt comforted to know that he would be there for Rachel.

The family was confused about a course of action. Do they chaperone Will and Rachel? Do they send Will away to school now instead of after the holiday? No one knew how to handle the couple's situation. It made for an uncomfortable winter. Elizabeth and Betsy were always watching the two. Their husbands agreed that once Will went to school their problem would be solved. It was going to be an interesting holiday season for both sides of the family.

Chapter Four

The holidays were almost over and there was much to celebrate with the coming of Lizzy's wedding. Will and Rachel spend nearly every moment together but under the watchful eyes of Elizabeth and Betsy. There was much commotion in the Moore home during Christmas and it was easier for the cousins to meet in secret. But there would always be someone who would spoil their brief intimate visits.

Then came the sad day when Will would have to leave South Carolina. He assured Rachel that during the summer hiatus he would return and hoped the family would be more open to their relationship. They only had this last day together to say goodbye. They walked down to the riverside. The air was crisp, and dusk was falling. And in the shadow of the old oak tree covered in silvery Spanish moss that gently waved in the wind, they kissed one last time.

Lizzy had just accompanied some guests out to their carriage when she noticed Rachel and Will off in the distance. She had not been privy to the news of Rachel and Will. She had been much too busy preparing for her nuptials which would take place in early Spring. She went to call out but noticed their close embrace. She was a little surprised and upset by this event. She would have to confront her sister later once all the guests had left. Lizzy was happy the festivities were over. She was feeling tired and not herself. She decided to let the matter rest and as soon as everyone had gone, she went straight to bed.

Unfortunately, Lizzy would not leave her bed again. The next morning, she found herself too exhausted to leave her chamber. The family believed she had just overexcited herself the night before and needed to rest. But over the next few days, her breathing became shallow. Elizabeth noticed Lizzy had a fever and immediately asked John to fetch the town doctor. Once he saw Lizzy's condition, he told the family the news. Lizzy had influenza. There had been a worldwide epidemic in the early 1760s and the doctor was afraid another serious outbreak would occur again.

The doctor told the Moore's he had seen more than one case lately and believed it was brought in by newcomers to the city. He was afraid it would spread fast and told the Moore's that Lizzy would have to stay in her room, no sunlight, or open windows. He would come by and check on her when he could. But no one was to visit her except one caretaker, whomever they chose to watch over her.

Of course, Elizabeth stepped up to take care of Lizzy. The home was quarantined and she had to keep the rest of her children away from the house until Lizzy got well. So, John went to Charles Town to give the Neufville's the news. Betsy and Johnathon were more than happy to help and ask that the family stay with them until all was well. They had room now that Will and another son Isaac had gone off to school.

But news spread of the local sickness and within a few days Billy Allston came to their home. Elizabeth heard him knocking repeatedly on the front door. She placed a cool cloth on Lizzy's forehead and went to answer it. She only opened the door a crack. Billy asked to enter, but Elizabeth would not allow it. She did not want Billy to become ill. As she started to shut the door, he placed his foot inside the doorway so Elizabeth could not close it.

"She is to be my wife. Although we have not recited our vows, I am stepping in to care for her as her husband. Please, sweet lady, allow me to enter."

Elizabeth is moved by his words and allowed Billy entry. He rushed up the staircase and hurried into Lizzy's room. It was still and dark even on a sunny day. The heavy curtains had been drawn and no light entered. He scarcely recognized his bride to be. He could see she was much thinner, and her eyes had dark shadows beneath them. She was as pale as ivory. He gently bent down and whispered her name. She did not respond. He called a little louder and removed the cloth from her forehead. She was bathed in sweat. She slowly opened her eyes. A tiny smile emerged, and she whispered his name in response. Billy took the handkerchief from his jacket pocket and wiped her glistening brow. He held her tiny hand and stayed by her side throughout the night.

Elizabeth stayed in the outdoor seating area. She did not enter the room for many hours. Hopefully if she saw Billy, it would lift her spirits and help her become well again. In the early morning hours, Elizabeth left to draw water from the well and bring it back upstairs. She gently opened the door and saw Billy on the bed beside Lizzy. His head was in his hands as he softly wept and repeated Lizzy's name. But as Elizabeth walked closer, she realized that her daughter was barely alive. Elizabeth slowly fell to her knees by her bed, spilling the pitcher of water. Lizzy turned her head towards her mother and smiled. She gazed back at Billy and without even a whimper took her last breath. Elizabeth could not move. Only a flood of tears streamed from her face. She inhaled a huge breath and cried out as loud as she could. Billy softly reached for Lizzy's hands and placed them over her heart. He bent over Lizzy and gently kissed her forehead. He lifted himself up and helped Elizabeth off the floor. She had no strength in her legs and became unsteady on her feet. All he could do was hold Elizabeth tightly and let the mother of his fiancée cry for her beloved daughter.

After spending the rest of the morning with Elizabeth, Billy made the ride back to Charles Town. He told Elizabeth he would stop at the Neufville's home and give them the sad news of Lizzy's passing. He did not rush back to the city. He needed some time to digest what had just occurred. Once he reached Neufville's front door it took him a few moments before he could knock. He wanted to compose himself before entering with such terrible news.

Rachel heard a horse approaching and looked out the window. She saw Billy dismount and watched as he stood motionless at the door and wondered why he had not knocked. She walked through the main hall and opened the door. Billy stood before her; his head hung low. When he managed to raise his eyes, she saw how red they were from tears. She was about to ask if he knew about Lizzy's condition but by the look on his face, she already knew the answer. He slowly stepped through the door but could not make a sound. Rachel knew her sister was gone. She shook her head back and forth repeatedly in disbelief. It could not be possible. Not Lizzy. Not her sister.

Rachel felt lightheaded and turned to sit in a chair. Billy took her by the arms and held her. She did not want his embrace. But she was too distraught to fight or pull away. She simply gave in. Not a single word was spoken between the two. They held each other until they heard Rachel's siblings come into the room along with Betsy. Betsy looked at Billy and asked for the reason for his visit. He finally had the words to express his sympathy and told them of Lizzy's last moments.

The family knew they had to get back to Elizabeth quickly and console her. But John Moore had not heard of his daughter's passing. Billy agreed to escort the family back to Rachel's home and then would go seek John at his workplace.

Rachel was moved by Billy's actions. She was surprised to see another side to this gentleman. Over the course of many days, Billy helped the family in any way he could. When Elizabeth was ready to talk about Lizzy's last fleeting moments, Rachel heard of Billy's courage, his kindness and how he remained by her sister's side and comforted her mother. But one thing Rachel did not know was that Billy had been a widower before. His first wife passed away from a deadly fever and losing Lizzy was a terrible blow to Billy. Maybe Rachel was wrong about him.

In the following days, Rachel and the family prepared for Lizzy's funeral. Her tiny, pale body was dressed in what would have been her wedding gown. The gown had been Elizabeth's wedding dress and she had been working on it for many weeks as a gift for Lizzy to wear on her wedding day. The wake was held at the family home in Lizzy's bedroom. Black bereavement fabric was draped throughout the house and every mirror was covered. The local cabinet maker procured the wooden coffin and brought it to the home. The minister of their church along with family members and friends came throughout the night to give final prayers and condolences to the family. Elizabeth spent the entire night by Lizzy's bed constantly rearranging her dress or combing her hair. She still had not come to grips with the fact her child was dead. Betsy made sure visitors would be tended to and the husbands gathered in the downstairs parlor to accept condolences from the parade of guests. Chloe watched over the remaining children and kept them busy so Elizabeth could take time to mourn.

Rachel stayed in the corner of Lizzy's bedroom and watched the candles cast shadows on the walls. She was concerned for her mother. She would not eat no matter what was offered. As the last of the evening's mourners left the room, Rachel heard a voice speak softly to her and noticed someone's hand with a small cordial glass of brandy. It was Billy offering her some spirits to ease her during this time. She declined at first, but Billy offered it again. She accepted the glass and drank a good deal of the brandy. She was not used to libations but felt she needed something to comfort her. She turned to Billy, handed the glass back and nodded. He gave a small bow in return and stood by her side the rest of the evening. There they both stood and watched the candles flicker until they extinguished in the early morning light.

Mid-morning, they left and escorted Lizzy to her final resting place. There was the look of exhaustion on everyone's face. It was a cold, misty day; cloudy and depressing. The men of the family lined up to take the casket down the street to the church yard. John, Jonathon, and Billy took their stations as pall bearers while the women followed down the road. It would be a long walk on an even longer day.

The ceremony ended just as night was about to fall. Billy accompanied the family to their home and gave a final condolence before he would leave for his home in Murrells Inlet. Before he left, Rachel thanked him for his kindness and dedication to her sister. She told him how thoughtful he was during this heavy time and how well he carried on the role of husband although he and Lizzy were not legally married.

Billy bowed and told Rachel, "Whether you believe it or not, I did care for your sister. I also admire your family, especially your mother, who has gone through an incredibly trying time. And, of course, for you Rachel. I hope you can see there is a gentleman beneath my rugged and rough exterior. I have a great deal of respect for your family...and for you."

Rachel tilted her head and blushed. Billy mounted his horse, tipped his hat, and rode away. Rachel watched as he rounded the corner and headed north. From then on Rachel would give him the title of Gentleman Billy.

With the funeral over and mourners gone, the family had time to themselves. Rachel did not know if anyone had written to Will to tell him the sad news. She sat at her desk and wrote a letter to him explaining the terrible loss. She was still emotional and stopped many times to wipe away her tears. She ended her letter with the words, 'Forever yours, Rachel.' She wished Will had been there to help her through her sorrow. This was one time she desperately needed her best friend.

Many weeks passed and the Moore's would try to regain a sense of normalcy. Elizabeth would wear her black mourning dress every day. She stayed in mourning for months. She neither joked nor smiled with the rest of her children. She thought it was disrespectful to Lizzy's memory. It took a toll on her, and the role of homemaker would go to Chloe.

John knew this would be the best time to find Cubby and bring her home to help. It took him a few days to locate her and soon she was on her way back to Charles Town. He hoped this would make life easier for both his wife and bring Abraham some comfort. Abraham worked hard for the family, and John understood what it was like to lose a daughter.

Once John and Cubby reached his home, John rode straight towards the carriage house. Earlier in the day, John instructed Abraham to wait for him there when he returned from picking up supplies. Once John pulled up, Abraham heard the horses and walked outside. He did not recognize the other passenger in the carriage.

John smiled at Cubby. She softly said, "Poppa, it's me."

Abraham froze. Then a huge grin stretched across his face. Cubby jumped off the carriage and into her father's arms. Abraham spun his daughter around in circles until both were dizzy. John stepped off the carriage and watched as father and daughter were reunited. Abraham repeatedly thanked John for bringing his daughter back to him. John said he would give them a few minutes alone to catch up. Afterwards, it would be time for Cubby to learn the routine here at his plantation. Abraham nodded and took Cubby in his arms and spun her around again as they laughed and giggled. It had been a long time since John felt compelled to do something good other than make money. He imagined Lizzy looking down from Heaven. God, he wished Lizzy were in his arms. But as he watched Abraham and Cubby embrace, their reunion took a close second.

Rachel was close by and saw the commotion occurring by the carriage house. She walked closer and saw Abraham's smile from ear to ear as he spun a young girl in his arms. She wandered over to her father and took his arm. John smiled down at Rachel and began an introduction. Abraham suddenly stopped his playfulness and placed Cubby back on the ground. Cubby gave a small curtsey and held her head down so she would not look Rachel in the eye.

"This is Abraham's daughter, Cubby. I can only assume that it is her given name. She will be working in the main house helping Chloe. She will also be giving you as well as your siblings any assistance. Including your bereaved mother. God only knows she needs support during her melancholia."

Rachel gave a small smile to Cubby, but Cubby still held her head down. Rachel walked around the girl and Cubby continued to look towards the ground. Rachel offered to show her around the house and introduce her to her siblings. John told Abraham that he and Cubby would have more time to talk later that evening. It was time to give Cubby some instructions and introduce her to Elizabeth.

Cubby looked up towards her father. Abraham pointed to her, then to the house. She slowly walked along the trail with Rachel to the main house. She repeatedly looked back towards her father every few steps. She was feeling a little apprehensive the further she walked away from Abraham. Rachel noticed Cubby's hesitation and said that she should not worry. Rachel stopped before entering the house and made a promise to Cubby that she and her father, Abraham would never be separated ever again.

Cubby was shown around the house and introduced to Chloe. Chloe took Cubby by the hand and led her to the kitchen where she would be assigned to work most of the day. Then, Chloe took Cubby upstairs and towards the back bedroom. Chloe knocked on the door quietly. A voice told her to enter. It was Elizabeth. She was in Lizzy's room. As they entered the saw Elizabeth as she sat quietly in a rocking chair staring at the empty bed.

"Mizz 'Lizbeth, this here is Cubby. Mister John say I show her 'round da' house." Elizabeth briefly looked up at the two. She nodded and went back to her previous stare. Chloe quickly took Cubby out of the room and gently closed the door. Chloe sternly looked at Cubby and gave her a warning to never, ever go into this bedroom unless it were an emergency. And if she had to, knock first. You had to knock first. Cubby was a little confused but shook her head yes and did not question the rule. Both headed down the staircase and went about their chores. Cubby looked forward to spending time with her father later in the evening. And Abraham was anxious to tell his daughter what he had planned to do once he found out where his wife, her mother, had been taken.

Chapter Five

Springtime was in the air and warmer weather was upon them. Rachel spent her spare time writing letters to Will. He promised he would come home for a visit in the summer, and she looked forward to seeing him again. She wrote him how she and Cubby had spent much time together and she found her to be a comfort after Lizzy's death. She also mentioned her mother's melancholy and that she had not kept up with her sewing or needlework, which was very uncommon for her.

Every few days, she wrote to him. But she found it quite unusual that he did not return any of her correspondence. She asked her own family and the Neufvilles if they had heard anything from him, but everyone would give the same answer...no one had heard from Will, except Betsy. She told Rachel she had received a letter from Will when he arrived in Virginia where he expressed his willingness to stay at school and go straight into medical college so he may achieve his diploma quickly. This broke Rachel's heart. He had promised to come home during the summer months. Why hadn't he written and told her this himself? Was he having second thoughts about their relationship? Did he find someone else?

The late Spring brought many of the plantation owners and their families from the river and marsh regions to Charles Town to avoid the mosquitoes which caused disease such as malaria. The Allston's had a home in Charles Town and Gentleman Billy was with his family. Billy owned a racehorse named Trial and he had won quite a bit of money. Whenever he won money on the races Billy bought gifts for his family and friends including the Moore's. Billy stopped by many times to visit Rachel and the family. On occasion he would venture upstairs to visit Elizabeth who still stayed in Lizzy's room. But one particular day, he spent the better part of an hour with Rachel's mother. When he finally walked out of the room, Elizabeth came with him. It seemed like a miracle to them all. She was weak but had more presence of mind than the last few months. Rachel and the family rejoiced, especially John. They were happy to see their mother back among them. Little by little she would regain her strength and return to her daily routine. It was never quite clear why the sudden change or what was said between the two. But that would all come out soon enough.

Rachel continued to write to Will, but still no reply. She began to question whether Will was interested in another woman and that was his reason for not coming back. Betsy was close mouthed about her son and would only tell her he was busy with his studies and had truly little time for pleasantries and everyday gossip. This hurt Rachel's feelings. Were her letters nothing more than immature chatter to him?

But there had been letters from Will to Rachel. Elizabeth and John intercepted the correspondence and hid them from her. And when she sent a letter to Will, John gave instructions to the household servants to bring them to him or Elizabeth. They felt this was the only way to discourage the cousins from the idea of marriage.

By fall all correspondence stopped from Will and the families became concerned. Betsy no longer heard from Will and when they wrote to his school in Virginia they did not know Will's situation once he had left for England to study. The school in London had not responded to their request for Will's whereabouts.

One afternoon, while Rachel penned another letter to Will, Billy came by the Moore's home. He had just come from the racetrack and asked to see John Moore. He had something he wished to discuss with him. John was happy to fill his request and both men retired to John's office. After a brief period, John opened the door and asked Chloe to locate his wife so she may join their conversation. All the children were curious about this clandestine meeting and ran to find Rachel. By the time they found her and told her the news that Billy was meeting with their parents, she had an odd feeling. She quickly ran down the stairs towards her father's office. When the door opened, she found three smiling faces looking back at her.

"Ah, my daughter, what timing you have. Please step in. We have good news!"

Rachel took a few steps into his office. John quickly closed the door and walked over to Elizabeth while Billy stepped closer to Rachel. Her little heart pounded in her chest.

"Rachel, we have good news. Your father and I have accepted a proposal from Mr. Allston. He wishes to receive your hand in marriage, and we have accepted."

Rachel only stood and stared at them. She was without words. She gazed over at Billy with a confused expression on her face.

"My dear Rachel. I hope that you can see my intentions are good." But before Billy can finish his sentence, Rachel shakes her head in disbelief.

"I am sorry, sir. But my sister was to be your bride. It is only 6 months since her passing. I do not understand why I am chosen to take my sister's place?"

Elizabeth rose from her chair and walked toward her daughter.

"This gentleman has done our family a great service. We were filled with joy when he announced that he and our sweet Lizzy would be together in matrimony." Elizabeth started to cry. Billy handed her his handkerchief. Elizabeth wiped her tears and continued her statement. "But your father and I think both of you would make a great union. It is my wish that you marry Mr. Allston."

Rachel could not speak. She backed up toward the door and stumbled onto a chair. Billy walked to her and lowered himself on one knee. Her eyes widened and she held her breath.

"Rachel, I am asking you to be my wife. I have lost twofold and cannot bear to lose again." She could not answer. She felt she was backed into a corner without a way out.

Finally, her father spoke. "Rachel, it is a good union. This matter is done. Do not break your mother's heart. It is due to Mr. Allston that your mother is here by my side. When she was presented with the news of your engagement to him, she was brought back to us. She has been through enough and this is her wish."

Rachel crossed the room to her father, "But, what of my promise to Will?"

John looked toward his wife. Elizabeth stood and looked out the window as she looked for strength. She turned and approached Rachel. Billy stood up and took a few steps back.

"We did not wish you hear the fate of Will, for even we are not privy to the knowledge of his ...disappearance."

"Disappearance?" Rachel's voice quivered.

John and Elizabeth took Rachel to the sofa, neither of them wanted to tell her the news. John took it upon himself to answer her question. No one had heard from Will. According to Betsy and Jonathon, Will had gone to Virginia but his father had decided to send him to England to study medicine. They had received one letter from him before his voyage. Then all communication ceased. There had been no word from Will nor the school.

Rachel was horrified. She jumped up from the sofa and ran out of her home to the river. She stood motionless under the twisted oak tree where she last said goodbye to him. A torrent of tears streamed from her eyes. She could only repeat to herself that this cannot be. They were all wrong. He is still in this world. Rachel could feel it. He was not gone. He could not be gone.

Over the summer months there was still no news of Will's disappearance. Rachel would visit Besty at her home and asked if there was any information, but she was too sullen to speak. Betsy only shook her head and refused to talk any further.

During this period, Gentleman Billy would visit the family. He continued to ask Rachel for her hand, but she only turned her head and cried. One afternoon, Elizabeth called Rachel to her room. It was time a decision was made. Elizabeth made her plea once again that this was the best solution and that Rachel had to move on with her life. It was time she took Billy for her husband.

Rachel felt the pressure of both her family and Billy. She was tired and worn by their persistent harassment. She would finally relent. When Billy came to visit the following day, Rachel gave her answer... Yes.

Rachel asked that the wedding not occur until winter. She was still certain she would hear from Will again, but that day did not arrive. As autumn leaves fell, she knew the time had come to plan for the wedding. Her mother and Betsy made all the arrangements while Rachel waited for news from Will.

Winter was upon them, and a letter arrived at the Neufville home the day before Rachel and Billy's wedding. It was from a gentleman in London. It was about a young man they had at their hospital. He only gave his name as Will, and he lived in Charles Town. At first, they thought he was a resident of Virginia where his ship had sailed from. He had taken ill aboard ship with yellow fever. By the time it reached port in England he was unconscious. He had been with them for quite some time in and out of consciousness. Finally, they were able to gather his full name and information and sent word to the family of Will's condition.

Betsy and Jonathon were elated that their son was alive. But this made for a difficult decision between the Moores and Neufvilles. With the wedding only twenty-four hours away, both families decided it was best that Rachel not hear about the letter.

The next day Rachel and Billy married. Rachel was still in her teens, and Billy had been a widower with two children. Life would be completely different for Rachel. She would eventually move to Billy's plantation in Murrells Inlet just north of Charles Town. The plantation was named Brookgreen, and it was massive. Billy owned many slaves but as a wedding present, John sent Cubby to be with Rachel. Rachel was happy to have Cubby come with her, but she knew this would break the promise she had made to Cubby when they first met. So, as a sign of good faith, John allowed Abraham to go with Cubby. Little did anyone know there would be a surprise waiting for them when they reached the plantation.

When Rachel arrived at Billy's home, a servant greeted her at the door. It was Abraham's wife, Maryann. Rachel never knew Abraham's wife's name, so she did not make the connection. Abraham and Cubby were only a few steps behind Rachel when they saw Maryann. Cubby wanted to yell out to her, but they knew their place. They could not cause a commotion at the main house. That would spell trouble. They kept composed and waited till they all could meet later that evening at the servants' quarters. This was what Abraham had been praying for all these years. They were together again. And in time, they would be together as free people in the North.

It would take time for Rachel to settle down at her new house and she found that plantation life would be exhausting work. It would also get quite lonely. Her position at the plantation was to educate Billy's children from his previous marriage and eventually their children. She must also mend garments, give a list of instructions to the servants regarding daily chores, take care of the sick and many other tasks. There would not be many visitors to the plantation during summer months especially. The mosquito problem was unbearable in this region and many owners would go to the mountains or the shore. Billy had built a small but delightful cottage along the shore in an area between DeBordieu Beach and Pawleys Island. This was a small paradise to Rachel. She spent hour after hour walking along the sand as she watched ships head out to sea. She was thankful for the ocean breezes that kept them cool during the ungodly humid nights.

There was another reason Rachel enjoyed the shore. She was with child. The cool breezes helped her feel more comfortable during this time. She was quite excited but also very anxious. She had written to her mother about the blessed event and hoped she would come to the plantation to help her. Elizabeth would be more than happy to help with the newborn and eventually travelled to their home.

But Rachel would have trouble with the pregnancy and lost the little girl while in her seventh month. Billy was saddened by the news of the death and Rachel became despondent for months. Billy began to drink more and would disappear for days to Charles Town to gamble. Rachel became lonelier as time went by. She would make the trip to Charles Town to see the family during the heat of summer, but once the seasons changed, she had to go back to her duties on the plantation.

But things would become even more difficult due to the declaration of war. Each time Rachel would visit Charles Town there was a heavy presence of British soldiers. The British tried to keep the colonists under their control, but many settlers became outspoken against the monarchy. And her family would be amid the uprising.

The merchants and plantation owners of South Carolina decided along with the other colonies to turn against Great Britain. John Moore was elected senator for St. Thomas Parish and held a seat in the newly established Provincial Congress. Jonathon Neufville also held a seat at Congress and became the Commissioner of Loans for the state. It was up to them to raise money for the cause. They gained these seats from a small conflict earlier in 1775. The colonists had heard the news of the Boston Tea Party where their brethren disguised themselves as natives and crept upon a vessel in the Boston harbor. There they destroyed thousands of pounds of tea in the river. So, when Rachel's family heard a ship laden with tea was in their harbor, they confiscated it and hid it in the local jailhouse. This was a dangerous act against the crown and Rachel was nervous about the lives of her father and uncle.

And there were times when she thought of Will, that he would be a doctor or surgeon by now. He would have tended to the sick and she would have been by his side. It still saddened her that no word was ever heard from him. And even stranger how no one in the family spoke of him. At least, not around her.

But there had been word from Will. He still wrote to his parents but also sent correspondence to Rachel's family home. Elizabeth felt guilty for not informing Rachel that he was still alive and had written to the family. But she did not know the correct time to tell the truth about Will to Rachel. It would be Betsy's position to tell Rachel that he had overcome his illness, completed his studies, and was headed back to the states. He could not stay in Britain during these tumultuous times and felt he was needed here to take care of the soldiers of war. And in all the correspondence that Will sent, he continued to ask how Rachel had been and apologized for not writing before. Neither family could tell Will of Rachel's marriage to Billy. They only wrote that she was well and told him of other events in the city. They knew once he was back in South Carolina he would want to see Rachel. This would be a tricky situation for both families.

The country would be thrown into war, and it needed men desperately to fight the British. Will's brothers, who were of age, joined the fight. Betsy's family had been torn apart by the revolution. Elizabeth's only son, Rachel's brother would also join the war effort. And during it all, Will made it back to Charles Town. He could not wait to see his Rachel. But the first stop was at his parent's home. They were incredibly happy to see their boy home. They brought him food and drink to toast his homecoming. He hugged his parents repeatedly and asked if they knew if Rachel was at her home. He wished to see her the next morning.

His parents' smiles faded, and they told Will that Rachel was not home in Charles Town. That she had moved to Murrells Inlet. Will was a little perplexed. Why was she in Murrells Inlet? Had the whole family moved there?

His father took him by the shoulders and finally confided in his son. They explained that Rachel had married Gentleman Billy.

Will asked his father again about Rachel. His father repeated that Rachel was Billy's wife. He explained that the family had not heard from Will for many months, and convinced Rachel to go on with her life. It was at her parents' bidding that she married Billy.

Will would not believe it. He would have to see for himself. Will sat back in his chair, his eyes grew red. Not because of tears, but anger. Of all the people in the world why did she choose Billy?

Will picked himself up from the chair and bolted out the door. He had to talk to the Moores. He had to know why Rachel had betrayed him.

Will jumped on his horse and galloped towards the Moore's home. His parents called out to him, but he had not heeded their demands to come back. It would be nearly dark when he arrived at Rachel's family home. He hastily dismounted, ran towards the door, beating on it repeatedly.

When Rachel's father John answered he was shocked. He held his chest and stepped back. "Will, my boy! By all means do enter. Mrs. Moore will be so pleased to see her nephew again!"

Will pushed John aside and asked for Rachel. Elizabeth heard his voice and entered the hall. She was not prepared to see Will. She gasped and started to faint. Both men approached Elizabeth and offered assistance; each took an arm and walked her to a chair. She took a deep breath and excused herself. She looked again at Will and noticed the unhappy expression on his face.

Will spoke first and apologized for his forceful entry. He had to see Rachel. He had to know the truth.

Elizabeth and John repeated the same words his own parents used. That no one had heard from him for many months, and the family feared Will had met with some tragedy. Will then begged them to tell why she married Billy. But all they could say was it was a family decision and that the matter was over.

Will turned and walked toward the door. He tipped his hat towards John and Elizabeth and left their home speechless. All he could do was go back to his family home and decide what his next move should be.

The next morning, Will awakened and decided there was only one more thing to do. He must find Rachel and hear from her own lips why she surrendered to Billy. He left early at sunrise and made the trip north to Murrells Inlet.

Chapter Six

Will made the journey to Murrells Inlet and discovered the location of Brookgreen Plantation. It was a vast land surrounded by a lush green marsh to the east, and to the west flowed a river with fields of rice growing throughout. The Greek Revival mansion greeted visitors with a long avenue of oak trees. He knew it would come as a shock to Rachel to see him at her front door and he was nervous to have a confrontation with Gentleman Billy. He thought it would be wise to witness the home from a distance and see if he could catch Rachel alone.

He became more anxious as he watched servants come in and out of the mansion. His anger had not diminished, and he attempted several times to approach the front door. But he stopped himself each time. But as the afternoon passed, he knew he had to confront Billy. But just as he summoned the courage to walk up the avenue, he spotted Rachel. He ducked behind one of the trees. He peered around it and saw his love. Then suddenly he noticed Rachel was expecting. She was pregnant. He leaned against the tree for support. His eyes welled up with tears. He could not confront Billy nor Rachel.

He glanced around the tree one more time and watched her walk back inside the home. She paused for a moment and looked out toward the avenue. Then, she stepped inside. He received his answer. She had moved on with her life.

Will aimlessly walked back to his horse and began the long trip back to Charles Town. He was in no hurry to return. What did he have to go back to? He lost what was most important to him.

He continued to ride his horse toward a small port city named Georgetown and hoped he could find shelter there before he continued his journey home. Sad and alone, Will made it to Georgetown. He walked into the first tavern he found and asked for lodging and food. The owner graciously helped Will to a table and offered him a cistern of ale. Will continued to drink through the evening and had not spoken a word to any of the elderly patrons who had gathered there. But he overheard their conversations. They talked about the war and how young men were needed. There was talk of British soldiers who recently looked for patriots who hid in the woods nearby. The name Marion was mentioned several times. For days, the British had looked for Marion and his marauders in the forest and swamps. Will listened as they talked about the brave advances Marion had made for the country.

Their stories stirred something inside Will. It was time for him to start his life. After all, he had gone to medical school. He decided that night he would enter the war effort. He would immerse himself in his work. It was all he had left.

Will signed up for service the next day. He decided not to go to Charles Town but go straight to the front where doctors were needed. He eventually wrote to his parents to let them know he was bound for an area northwest of Charles Town called the Cowpens to help heal the soldiers. Little did he know how horrid and gruesome his task would be.

Will was acquainted with the regional diseases that would affect the men, but he was not quite ready for the challenges of surgery. Day after day he was bombarded with the shouts and cries of men in pain. Their writhing bodies brought in one after the other. Some days there was no end in sight. On occasion, he would have a respite for a few hours, but it was difficult to sleep with the sound of cannon fire in the distance. He heard gunshots in the nearby woods and knew he would be called back to duty. His blood-soaked clothes were rarely washed. There was little time to shave. His beard and mustache grew quickly with hints of grey throughout. He was no longer the little boy that took care of injured birds. He had the lives of brave patriots to mend.

Will devoted himself completely to the army. He was looked upon as a great doctor and the men were grateful for his service. But sleep did not come easy for him. He heard the cries of men as they called out to him in his dreams. He would wake suddenly and find himself drenched in sweat. And then there were times when he would dream of Rachel. But not dreams of their younger days but nightmares of the future. He had terrible nightmares. Rachel was in danger. A sudden hurricane had hit the coast of South Carolina. Rachel was on the beach and was taken by surprise by a rogue wave. She was drowning. Drowning and crying out for him; her outstretched hand above the waves. Will reached out to her but she froze when she saw him and refused to take his hand. She drifted beneath the water and out of his reach. This nightmare repeated over and over. He knew one day he would have to find his way back to Rachel. Somehow, someday.

But it may be some time before Will would ever see his Rachel. During a skirmish in the neighboring town, Will and other soldiers were captured and taken as prisoners of war. Will and the others were forced to march northeast into North Carolina and were held captive by the British for nearly 10 months. Will was the only doctor at the camp and had to attend to both patriots and British soldiers. His body would become weak from lack of food, but his will remained strong. He vowed he would get through this and find his way back home.

The majority of men he attended to died not from injuries of war but mostly from diseases such as yellow fever and dysentery. They would be given only stale bread and water once a day if it were available. The British took some men for questioning and returned them broken and bleeding. The loyalists treated Will better than some of the other prisoners. The enemy needed his powers of healing too. There were times the men fought over the last piece of bread. Small cuts became serious injuries that would become infected. And for the dying, there was nothing Will could do for them but make their last moments as comfortable as possible. Others had lost their minds and wandered around the camp aimlessly. Will felt his own mind slip into periods of deep depression. But his persistent dreams of Rachel kept him going. He felt he must stay alive for her.

In 1779 while Will was held by the British, Rachel was at Brookgreen and gave birth to a baby boy. Billy and Rachel named him Washington after the commander and chief George Washington. Billy was ecstatic to have a child after losing their first two. Not long after the birth of his son, Billy made the decision to join the army as well. Rachel was upset that he left her and the baby alone. And the entire operation of the plantation would be up to her as well. Billy explained it was his duty to help the cause. He heard that the colonists had made headway in the war. He presumed the conflict would end soon and he would be home in no time.

Rachel was not the only person upset by this decision. Abraham was too. Billy decided he would take Abraham with him as his servant. Because of Billy's connections and wealth, he would be given the title of Captain and was allowed to bring his servant with him. This outraged Abraham. He hoped when Billy left for war, he and his family would have a chance to escape. This destroyed his chances of being a free man. Abraham would have to think of another plan.

A couple of months after Washington's birth, Billy and Abraham left Brookgreen. Billy was given his assignment by his superiors. He would be under the command of Francis Marion who needed men in the Georgetown/Charles Town area. They were to replace the men that were captured earlier that year. Billy felt good to have a position close to home and was hopeful the war would end soon.

But many months would pass, and the war was about to enter the 1780s. And Abraham lost his patience. He had to devise a plan to leave soon. He thought with the commotion of gunfire and cannons he would have a chance to leave. But how would he get his family out? He thought of one solution. He had to force Billy to give up his commission and go back to Brookgreen. And there was only one way to make Billy leave.

In North Carolina, Will and his fellow soldiers received some incredible news. The British, who also lost many soldiers due to casualties, announced a prisoner exchange. The British chose Will and his men to be freed and sent back to Charles Town. The news was a godsend. Will's depression had run deep, and this renewed his spirit. The exchange occurred the next day and the men were sent back to duty. At least, those who were healthy enough to return to their posts. And Will was asked to perform his duties as surgeon once again for the patriots. He wanted more than anything to leave the service, but he felt duty bound and agreed to continue as chief surgeon for his regiment.

Will and the other soldiers were not sent back to the Cowpens but south towards the Georgetown region. And back to the chaos of battle. Will was under great stress with the number of men dying all around him and faced the gruesome task of amputating limbs. He had become more skilled as time passed, and the men knew they were lucky to have him. He worked tirelessly. And when he was given time to rest, the dream of Rachel haunted his slumber. He prayed for the day when his assignment would be finished, and he could return home.

One morning at 6am Will awoke to a terrible sound. There was an incredible amount of cannon fire nearby. Marion's men scurried throughout the nearby woods. Gunfire echoed all around the encampment. Before Will had time to wash, he was surrounded by wounded. They came from all sides. He only had a few instruments to work with and little gauze to wrap their wounds. Many injured men would have to wait hours for medical attention.

Soldiers at the camp could not locate their captain to give them word of the current situation. Cannon fire had moved closer, and they needed his order to retreat. The men found the captain in front of his tent. He complained of chest pains and collapsed in front of them. The men found Abraham in the tent and asked what had happened. Abraham could not explain his master's illness. They insisted Abraham carry the captain to the doctor's tent.

Will heard a familiar voice from outside the tent and recognized it immediately. It was Abraham. But when Will walked towards him, he noticed Abraham did not recognize him. Will had grown a full grey beard and mustache while he was imprisoned. His face was weathered. He no longer looked like the healthy young man he once was in Charles Town. He knew Abraham worked for his Uncle John and wanted to ask for news of the family, but he hesitated when he noticed the man Abraham carried in his arms. It was Billy. Abraham walked into the tent and asked for help.

"My massa be sick...very sick."

Will looked quickly at Billy's face. He was pale and showed signs of jaundice. Billy moaned from pain but did not recognize Will. Will did not utter a word, his cheeks flushed with anger. Here was the one man he did not ever wish to see again and here he was dying in front of him. Will gazed back at Abraham and told him he could not help him. He told Abraham to leave the captain on a cot outside the tent until he had taken care of other soldiers who were in more serious condition. Abraham did not argue and left Billy outside the tent. Abraham stood by Billy and watched the action that occurred around the encampment, the constant number of wounded flowed in and out. Will noticed that Abraham did not look overly concerned about Billy. Although Will knew Billy was deadly ill, he had too many soldiers to save. Men who were in dire need of attention. Billy would just have to wait.

By evening, Francis Marion arrived at camp and noticed the discomfort Captain Allston was in. He asked Will if Captain Allston was in fair condition or was anything further needed for his care. Will reluctantly walked back to face Billy. He was weaker and could not control his vomiting. Billy seemed confused when he tried to speak to Marion, but his words made no sense. Marion asked to see Will alone. Before they left, Will instructed Abraham to give Billy water and watch over him.

As Will and Marion walked into the tent to discuss other soldiers' needs, Will noticed Abraham with a small pouch in his hand. He sprinkled something into a cup and added water from a pitcher sitting inside the tent. He immediately offered the mixture to Billy. Once Abraham did this, he looked up and noticed Will had seen what transpired. It was then that Abraham recognized Will. He stood and nodded at Will. Will took a step forward toward Abraham but stopped. Abraham put his index finger up to his lips. Will took another step and took the cup from Abraham's hand. He held it to his nose; he knew that odor. Oleander. He understood what Abraham had done. Will looked away from Abraham and returned to the tent to speak to Marion. He hesitated for a moment, then looked Marion in the eyes.

"I believe the captain is experiencing trouble with his heart. There is nothing I can do for him here. It would be best to send him home. I do not think he has much time left on this earth."

Marion agreed with Will and commanded Abraham to pack the captain's things and take him back to Brookgreen. Will excused himself and walked back with Abraham to Billy's tent. They both stood across from each other. Will held out his hand. Abraham extended his. While they shook hands, Will instructed Abraham to tell the family of Billy's 'heart condition'...and to continue to give him water along the way home. Abraham nodded his head. Both men understood each other completely. Abraham knew he might be questioned by the family. He asked what if the family required the doctor's name. Will played with his beard while he thought for a moment. He then told Abraham, "If they question you, tell them the physician's name was Doctor Grey."

Captain Billy Allston was placed into a small cart and Abraham gathered his things and started for the journey home to Brookgreen. Will watched as they both drove away. He bowed his head, unsure of the deed he had just been an accomplice to. This was not like him. He had taken a vow and he let his heart overrule his head. He knew Billy would not survive much longer. Not if Abraham continued his course of action.

Days later Marion's men would be sent to a skirmish in Savannah, Georgia. This was not what Will had hoped for. He wanted to learn the fate of Billy and now he would be miles away from his home...and Rachel. Maybe it was better he did not know the fate of his rival.

Abraham made the drive towards Brookgreen. He knew there would be trouble if anyone found the pouch on his person. Before he reached the gates, he threw the poison into a hollow tree. He rode the horse and cart up the long, tree lined avenue and looked for his wife and daughter. But the first person he encountered was Rachel. She heard the cart approach and darted for the door. When she reached the bottom step of the porch she waved to Abraham, encouraging him to come straight to her. She swung her head around and looked for Billy but did not see him.

Abraham pulled alongside the step where Rachel stood and slowly said, "I sorry Miss Rachel, but there nuttin' I coulda dun. Capt'in Allston awful sick. A doctor name Grey say he gots a bad heart." He then pointed to the back of the cart. Rachel ran behind the cart and held her hand up to her face. She let out a small cry and pulled Billy towards her. Billy was unconscious. She yelled to Abraham to help her bring him to his bed chamber. Abraham did as he was instructed and took Billy upstairs to his room. Once Abraham set Billy down in his bed, he left to find his family. This is the moment he had waited for. This was his time to leave and find freedom.

Abraham found Maryann and Cubby at the back of the house fetching water from the well. Maryann ran to hug him, but he took her by the arms and instructed her to listen to him carefully. She listened quietly. Tonight was the night they would run. Abraham explained how he had given Billy something in his drink and Billy was extremely ill. Maryann asked Abraham what he gave Billy and if he were only sick, or could it get worse? Abraham did not go into detail. He explained that Rachel would be too busy nursing Billy through the night. Abraham instructed Maryann to take the water upstairs. While Maryann helped Rachel, Abraham and Cubby would pack their things. Maryann had to meet them back at the well and all three would run throughout the night. They had to put a lot of distance between themselves and the plantation before anyone realized they were missing.

Maryann did as she was told and took the pitcher of water to Rachel. Rachel thanked her and began to cry. Maryann genuinely felt sad for Rachel. Although she had not thought kindly of Billy, she did feel sympathy for her mistress. Rachel told her that Captain Allston would need quiet, and she could leave. It was up to Rachel to nurse Billy. There were no available doctors in the area due to the war and she was left alone to care for him. There was nothing she could do but apply cold compresses to Billy's forehead and pray.

Rachel stayed by Billy's side throughout the night and read the bible aloud for him to hear. During the early morning hours, Billy woke. He whispered Washington's name and Rachel raced across the hall to bring her son to Billy. Billy looked at his son's tiny face and uttered a prophecy. "He who lives to see him grow up will see a great man." Then, his voice ceased, and he fell unconscious. Rachel continued to place cold cloths on his forehead and read from her bible. An hour passed, and Billy opened his eyes. Rachel smiled at him and whispered his name. He uttered one word to her...water. She assumed he wanted a drink. She poured a glass of water and pressed it to his lips. But he immediately pushed it out of her hand and passed out. She could not understand why he did this. She picked up the glass and began to read the bible again. At sunrise, while the mourning doves cooed on the bedroom windowsill, Captain Billy Allston passed away.

Rachel was exhausted. She felt she had failed to save her husband. After a few moments of tears, Rachel raised herself from her chair. Her son Washington had fallen asleep in her lap. When she left Billy's room and walked across the hall to place Washington in his bed, she realized how quiet the home was. There was no movement, no chatter, no one met her at her chamber. She left Washington in his bed and called out to Cubby. No response. Then Maryann. Again nothing. She would ask another servant where they both were. The servant only shrugged her shoulders. By mid-morning, the answer was clear. All three were gone.

Rachel sent word of Billy's death to his cousins. They lived at the neighboring plantation and were first to arrive at Brookgreen a couple of hours later. It took some time to reach a local justice to inform them of Billy's demise. Little by little, other family members arrived over the following week. Rachel was not prepared to be a widow at such a youthful age. She was already overwhelmed with acres of rice and indigo to harvest along with numerous slaves to manage. In the days that followed, she contacted her family and was grateful they could help her manage her affairs. It was a blessing that they were there and helped guide her through her grief. Rachel also had the uncomfortable job of finding Abraham and his family. She had been betrayed. She thought of all her servants, she could trust Cubby. They were inseparable during her confusing teen years. She was more of a friend than a servant. But this was a difficult lesson for her to learn. From now on she learned to trust no one.

Captain Billy Allston's funeral was a small affair. British soldiers were still present in the area and anyone who travelled to and from could find the route dangerous. Only Rachel's immediate family as well as Billy's cousins paid their respects. Billy would be buried in the family plot only yards away from the river. The river that gave them so much wealth. The place where Spanish moss hung on giant oaks like grey ghosts and waved gently in the breeze. They waved as if to say good-bye to Gentleman Billy.

Chapter Seven

Time dragged on for Rachel throughout the coming year. She had learned to be a strong woman, determined to keep the plantation efficient and profitable. According to Billy's will she had obtained the rights to all possessions on the plantation along with the summer beach cottage on Pawleys Island. Rachel was content to raise Washington alone, but it came at a cost toward the end of the war.

British soldiers had advanced into the Murrells Inlet area and took residence at Brookgreen. They took food and livestock for their own and left little for Rachel and the plantation workers. General Cornwallis himself found the plantation to his liking and brought his commanding officers with him to use Rachel's home for their headquarters. This infuriated Rachel. How dare they set foot on her property. But she was in no position to argue. She had a small child, and they could easily arrest them both. Or worse, defile her and take her son away. So, when the soldiers arrived, she humbly welcomed them to her home and offered whatever they wanted. But at the same time, she would curse them under her breath. She played the gentile woman by day and prayed for their demise at night. There were even times when she walked to the river to Billy's grave and asked him for guidance. Maybe he still watched over them and could help them in some way.

At the end of the third day, General Cornwallis invited Rachel to join him for afternoon tea. She was gracious and accepted his invitation. Once the General heard Rachel had a son, he asked his name. Rachel smiled and happily replied that her son's name was Washington. Cornwallis was amused and asked to meet with this 'little general.' When Washington approached Cornwallis, he gave a small bow and proceeded to ask his mother why this man was sitting in his father's chair. Cornwallis was taken by the character of this child and instructed his men to pay respect to both the 'little general and his brave mother.' From there, Rachel and her son were no longer worried about their safety.

Within a few weeks, the end of the war was near, and the British would leave South Carolina. Over time friends of Billy's would come to visit only to find the head of the plantation was dead. When asked what took him, Rachel could only answer that the wage of war was harsh, and he had died fighting for his country.

Another friend of Billy's soon found his way to Brookgreen. Doctor Henry Collins Flagg had left the military and made his way through the countryside. He hoped to see his old friend Billy and the Allston family. Along the stretch of dirt road, he came across a servant hauling corn and asked if he was near Brookgreen and if he was acquainted with Captain Allston. The servant sadly gave the doctor the news that Captain Billy was no longer in this world, but his widow was still in charge of the plantation.

Doctor Flagg was saddened to hear the news and continued to the home to pay his respects to the widow Allston. Once at the plantation, he climbed down from his horse and knocked on the front door. This would be a tricky situation to introduce himself to the widow. He had never met her and hoped he did not bring her more pain during this grim time. A servant answered and he introduced himself. He asked if it was a suitable time to visit with the widow and pay his respects. She took his coat and hat and led him to the parlor. Henry looked around the spacious room. He noticed a painting of his friend Billy on the wall above the fireplace mantel. He stood and gazed at the portrait. He could not believe his friend was gone.

Henry heard the door behind him open. He spun around and was met by Rachel.

"I am Doctor Henry Flagg. I had come to visit my dear friend Captain Billy Allston but had heard before my arrival that he had passed. I am so terribly sorry for your loss, and I do hope I am not imposing at this most inopportune time."

Rachel held out her hand to greet Henry. Henry immediately took her hand and kissed it. Rachel had never met the doctor before and thought a visit from a friend of Billy's would make the day more palatable. For the rest of the day, they would regale stories about Billy. Rachel was happy to show the doctor around the plantation. There was an instant liking between the two and Rachel felt she could confide in Henry. In some ways, Henry reminded Rachel of Will. Tall in stature with gentle blue grey eyes. He had a soft kindness to his voice that gave her a sense of peace. He easily made her laugh and often apologized to her if he felt he had overstayed his welcome. Rachel told Henry that it had been some time since she had laughed and asked him to stay for dinner. During dinner Rachel said it would be an honor if he stayed as a guest for the night. He at first declined the offer. He did not want to impose. But Rachel insisted. She knew her husband Billy would have made the same offer, so she extended the invitation herself in her husband's place. Henry accepted the gracious invitation. It would only be the first of many.

The next morning Henry knew he must take his leave. Rachel thanked him again for his kindness and asked if he would come to visit her again. Henry was grateful for the time they had spent together and promised Rachel he would. Over the next year Henry and Rachel would spend many hours together on her plantation. Word had spread and some people felt it was too soon for Rachel to become involved with another gentleman after the recent death of her husband. But Rachel was young and to find a gentleman like Henry so much to her liking was good for her well-being. She had spent months in confinement on the plantation and did nothing but manage finances, slaves, schedules and raise a child. She felt it was time to go on with her life, no matter what people thought. Especially her family.

Word reached her parents in Charles Town regarding the recent sighting of Doctor Flagg at Brookgreen. They opposed the so-called friendship that had happened between them and were unhappy with

Doctor Flagg's background. He was a northerner. There were some issues between the politics of the north and the south. Now that the United States had won the war, there were arguments between the governing parties. A few tensions had started between those above and below the Virginia border. Although Dr. Flagg had an impressive record and was quite revered in the medical community it still did not change his place of birth. And Rachel's parents made special note of this subject, especially since both her father and uncle held political seats in South Carolina.

But Rachel continued to communicate with Henry. They would be seen throughout Murrells Inlet, Georgetown, and Charles Town on occasion. Their friendship would grow stronger over time and by 1783 Henry asked Rachel to be his wife. She happily accepted. Her family was quite upset with her and repeatedly asked that she rethink the matter

Rachel's final response would be, "My first marriage was to please my family. My second marriage is to please myself."

In 1783 Will Neufville is discharged from the army. His commission as chief surgeon is at an end along with the war. He was promised a great deal of land as a reward for his service, and he was anxious to claim his payment for services rendered. But his reward did not come. And that is true for many soldiers who stayed to fight to the end of the conflict. The newly formed Continental Congress had promised land in lieu of cash payment. They were still conforming to the new American dollar and ridding themselves of British currency. Will had looked forward to that land. It would help him start a new life without asking his parents for help.

But, even if he asked, his parents were almost destitute themselves. They, along with Rachel's parents, had loaned a considerable sum of money to the cause. It was Will's fathers' job to raise money in the form of loans for the American army but there was nothing to pay back to the citizens. Rachel's father had loaned the newly formed government over $16,000.00 himself and was extremely disappointed that he did not acquire one dime back at the end of the revolution. Each and every loan the colonists made to the local government was not paid back.

Will and his fellow soldiers were getting ready to leave Savannah, Georgia, and head back to Charles Town by ship. There were many soldiers from other camps who travelled with him on this voyage. One young man sat next to Will on the deck of the ship. They exchanged names and found out they both had family in Charles Town. The gentleman also mentioned a name he thought Will would remember... Captain Billy Allston. The young man asked if Will was the doctor in charge at the captain's camp and if he heard the sad news that Captain Billy had succumbed to his illness and passed away.

"Passed away?" asked Will, a little shaken by the news. "Last I saw Captain Allston he was taken home due to a heart ailment."

The young man repeated the news and apologized if he upset Will. Will shook his head and tried to change the subject. He was full of guilt but relieved. He now knew Billy was gone. And, just maybe, he had a chance once again to be with his Rachel.

As night began to fall along the Georgia coast, the wind began to pick up. The wind had changed direction and blew from the southeast. The ship pitched back and forth. The men felt in the pit of their stomachs that the seas were not in their favor. They were taken below deck where they huddled together. The ship creaked and moaned as it bounced from wave to wave. Many became seasick and Will was back on duty again. He himself would stay close to the hatch to breathe some fresh air and keep away from the nauseous odor.

As the tides grew higher and higher, the boat tossed side to side. The wind's high pitch whistle had gotten increasingly louder until it was almost deafening. No one could sleep. Will had started to shake with fear. His only thought was how he could get back to Rachel. And what about Rachel? Was she experiencing this tidal surge at her home? Was she alone and in fear? He remembered the nightmares he had as she reached out to him but sank under the undulating waves. How could he help her? How could he reach her?

Suddenly, the soldiers heard men above shout out commands. It did not sound as if the ship would make it to Charles Town but had run off course. They feared the ship would be tossed out to sea or run aground near Georgetown. The men could do nothing more than pray.

One man opened the hatch from the upper deck to shout out orders to the men below. Salty seawater flowed like a waterfall into the compartment. Men screamed and cried out for mercy from God. Will pulled himself up the ladder to help close the hatch but could not due to the powerful winds. He walked onto the deck and tried again to shut the hatch but was hit by a powerful wave. He and a handful of the crew aboard deck were thrown out to sea. As Will and the crew swam for the shore they watched as a rogue wave tossed the ship on its side. The cries of his fellow soldiers echoed over the thunder of the waves and into Will's ears. As the vessel began to sink, he could feel a tug from the undertow. He was being pulled back under the ship. Desperate to live, Will swam as hard as he could towards the distant lights on the shore. As he got closer to the beach, Will could no longer hear the howls of the men as the boat disappeared beneath the briny water.

Earlier in the day before the storm made itself known, Rachel had decided to spend time with her son and Dr. Flagg at her beachside cottage. Although it was quite windy in the morning, she felt it would help her stay cool from the unusually hot autumn day. The doctor had not arrived yet, so she decided to hold his dinner and read her favorite book to her son, Washington.

As Rachel read her story aloud to her son, she could hear the wind whistle as it picked up speed. She could hear the banging of the window shutter and went to see if she could fasten it tighter. The rain had just started, and she needed help from her servant to close it. She became a little concerned for Henry. It was no wonder he was late due to this sudden stormy weather.

Will continued to make his way to shore. He ingested much sea water, and his breathing was cut short each time he took a stroke. The only guiding light was a faint glow just off the beach. He knew he could make it. He had to. With what little strength he had left he made it to the darkened beach. The sand was whipping in his eyes and face which made it hard for him to see. He fell several times and ended up by the marsh reeds. He tripped and fell once more and found himself stuck in the pluff mud. He knew this could be trouble. He was familiar with the substance which could act like quicksand and pull a person under. He climbed through the grey mud and managed to make it back to level ground. He tried to wipe his eyes again. Mud covered his entire body. Exhaustion had taken its toll and he had difficulty breathing. His left side had been gouged by a branch beneath the mud and the wound was bloody and painful. If he could just reach the light, he could find someone to assist him.

Bloody and in pain he continued toward the light until he collapsed on the front porch of the home. He reached up to knock but could only pat softly upon it. He continued to pat until the door opened. A servant looked out and finally noticed Will lying on the ground. Will gazed up and asked the servant if he could see the master of the home and pled for shelter. The servant helped Will up and brought him in.

"Thar be no massa here, only Miss Rachel. I can fetch her."

Will could not believe what he had just heard. He looked the servant in the eyes and asked if it were Mrs. Rachel Allston who was the mistress of the home?

The servant answered, "Yes, but she won't be Allston fer long. She be Mrs. Flagg soon."

Will fell to his knees. The servant ran to fetch Rachel who had heard the commotion. She thought it was Henry and called out his name as she rounded the corner into the entry hall. Will picked himself off the floor. He was completely covered in grey mud, his beard and mustache caked. Rachel stopped in her tracks. She realized it was not Henry. She looked up and down at this man in horror completely covered in mud and blood. She looked again and then she recognized his eyes. It was his steel grey eyes that gave him away.

"Rachel!" Will cried out.

Rachel placed her hands over her mouth and quietly whispered the word, "Will" ... then fainted.

Both her servant and Will ran to her side. The servant turned to Will and insisted he not touch Rachel. Will proclaimed he was a physician and only wanted to help. The servant once again insisted Will not touch his mistress. While Will tried again to speak another figure walked through the door. It was Henry. He quickly rushed in, picked up Rachel and placed her on a small chair. He held her closely and turned towards Will.

"Who are you and what do you mean by frightening my future wife?"

Will could not answer Henry. He walked back through the door and into the storm. The hurricane had increased, and the winds whistled. Will suffered from shock and limped out into the storm. He was finished with life and all the disappointment he found in it. He continued toward the marsh unsure of his fate.

After a few tense hours, the morning light was a welcome sight. The night had brought much flooding and wind damage to the island as well as local plantations by the river. Henry and Rachel spent the night huddled by the fireplace. When she had woken from unconsciousness Henry asked who the gentleman was that came covered in mud. Rachel was confused and told Henry she thought it had been a dream. She told him she believed the man to be her cousin Will, but the family had not heard from him for so long and she herself thought he had passed away. Henry noticed the look of sadness in her eyes. She asked if Will was still in the home. Henry explained how the man left just after he questioned him and that he did not give his name. Rachel jumped up and went to the door. She opened it only to find debris and marsh reeds everywhere. Henry calmly took her by the shoulders and guided her back into the house. There was too much devastation, and it was not safe for her to venture out. Henry insisted he would look for Will as soon as they did inventory of what was lost during the storm.

Rachel begged Henry to look for Will. Henry sat her on a chair and told one of the servants to fetch Washington and bring him to her. When Washington entered the room Rachel scooped him up in her arms and cradled him. The toddler tried to push her away, he had slept through the worst of the storm to everyone's amazement. Rachel held him even tighter as tears fell from her eyes. Washington pulled away and looked up at his mother and quietly said, "Mother, do not cry. The grey man and I will protect you from the storm."

Rachel asked Washington what man he was referring to. Washington pointed out the door. Rachel assumed he was talking about Henry and hugged her son again.

Henry ordered the servants to help inventory anything that was damaged or lost in the storm. The only thing they could find missing was one of the horses. They assumed the winds had blown the stall door open and the animal would probably return in time. When they finished inventory, the home and all in it survived one of the strongest hurricanes the area had seen in many years. As Henry rode around the island, he noticed every home or cottage was torn apart. Every building on the island was a complete loss, yet by the grace of God their little cottage remained sound.

But as he and others on the island surveyed the damages no one mentioned seeing a man in grey in the area. Henry would have to report to Rachel that her cousin had not been seen but maybe he had found shelter from another family nearby. Rachel was terribly upset to think that her cousin may have met his fate out in the surge.

Once the cleanup had been completed, Rachel went out to the beach to look for Will. She wandered along the shoreline desperate to find any sign of her cousin. What she did find were the remains of a ship out in the inlet and along the beach. As she walked closer to the sand dunes, she noticed a piece of clothing peeking out of them. When she walked closer, she was horrified to see it was a sleeve with a swollen pale hand reaching out of it. She screamed and ran back to her cottage to retrieve Henry. Both rushed back to the beach and Rachel pointed to the gruesome discovery. Henry instructed Rachel to stand back and turn her head. As she did so, Henry dug the bloated body out. When he rolled him over, he realized it was not Will, but a sailor who must have worked on the ship that had crashed on the shore. He would not be the only body found during that week. Other bodies from the wreck washed ashore as well. And each time, Rachel would insist on seeing if it were her cousin. But Will was not among them.

Within a few days, their horse that had disappeared during the storm returned to the property. The animal was caked in grey pluff mud and there was dried blood along its flank. They examined the animal but could find no sign of injury. No one was sure just what had happened to the creature during the terrible hurricane.

Chapter Eight

Months had passed and there was no sign of Will. By January of 1784 Rachel wed Dr. Henry Flagg. Although she loved Henry and felt blessed to have married him, she still thought of Will and what type of life they may have had together. Rachel and Dr. Flagg moved back to Brookgreen and began their lives as husband and wife. Dr. Flagg owned a plantation near the Cooper River in Charles Town but was taken with the majestic beauty of Brookgreen and spent much of his time there. He continued with his medical practice in Charles Town and Rachel would come with him and stay in the city for a while. But she would always head back to Brookgreen. Her heart was there among the Spanish moss and sprawling oak trees. But mostly, her heart was at her little cottage on the beach at Pawleys Island. Henry's schedule would keep him in the city quite a bit, but he would reunite with Rachel on the sandy shore whenever he could.

Rachel was thrilled that Henry stepped up as a father for Washington. He doted on the boy and called him son. Over the years, Rachel and Henry had many children. The one thing Rachel genuinely wanted was a large family and the love of a devoted husband.

Rachel would give birth to four children. Two boys and two girls. They named the oldest after Henry, the next boy Ebenezer after Henry's father. They chose to name the oldest girl Rachel and the next Elizabeth after Rachel's mother. And their lives would be full and Brookgreen plantation would thrive.

Henry and Rachel would have more than just children at their plantation home. Henry had been the Surgeon General during the Revolutionary War and there was word that President George Washington was coming to the Waccamaw Neck for a southern tour to thank Dr. Flagg and other patriots for their service. He first visited his friends the Vereens in Little River and made his way south to Brookgreen in April of 1791.

Rachel was excited to meet the President, especially when she had the pleasure of introducing her son Washington to him. The President was quite honored that this lovely woman named her son after him. Rachel recited the story of when Cornwallis had stayed at her home during the war. When the President heard the tale, he laughed full heartily and wished he had been a fly on the wall to see and hear the event for himself. The President could only stay for one night, but it was quite a memorable one. He told the couple how impressed he was with the grounds and had never seen such beauty. He left at 6 am the next day to make his way towards Charles Town and bid his hosts goodbye. Henry and Rachel could not have been happier with their famous guest and reveled in telling the story to their family and neighbors for many years.

But soon after this historic visit when summer arrived, Rachel would go back to the little cottage on the shore of Pawleys Island. She sat among the wind-swept dunes and watched the waves pound against the sand. The cries of the gulls interrupted her daydreams of she and Will together. She sat for hours and waited for the day she would see him again. She still could not keep his memory from encompassing her thoughts. She would often lose track of time and had no idea how long she had been out on the beach until her children would comb the area to find her.

Henry noticed Rachel's behavior whenever summer and fall arrived. It was hurricane season, and he noticed his wife became more anxious when the skies darkened, and the clap of thunder could be heard in the distance. She knew it would be better to stay in Charles Town at Henry's plantation or the mountains during this time of year, but she was always drawn to the cottage on the shore. Henry told her it would not be safe to stay there when harsh weather approached, but Rachel felt safe there. For some reason, she knew that she would be protected.

Rachel's and Henry's marriage had been a happy one but in 1801 Henry took ill. He was only 58 years old, and Rachel would spend her days nursing her husband. There had been a dreadful outbreak of yellow fever in Charles Town since 1794 and Henry had dozens of patients throughout the city who had fallen ill. Each year the outbreak would spread further outside the city walls. The epidemic was as far south as New Orleans and traveled as far north as New York City.

The disease was a difficult one to bring under control. It would start with a cough and would become increasingly hard to breathe. Fevers would bring on hallucinations. The sick would be unable to hold down food or water. The experience was worse for the youngest children and the frail elderly.

Rachel rushed to be by Henry's side in Charles Town when she received word of his illness. She felt it best that the children stay at Brookgreen while she attended to Henry's needs. She spent every minute by his side. The typical doctor in him did not want Rachel to become ill, but she was stubborn herself and would not leave him. Within the week, Henry would take his last breath with Rachel by his bedside. Rachel had become a widow again. But this was different. She genuinely loved Henry and it would take many months for her to begin life again without him.

Henry would be buried in Saint Thomas Parish near their plantation in Charles Town. It was a huge affair. Many people owed their lives to Dr. Flagg and wanted to pay their respects. Rachel had lost her parents 10 years earlier, but her siblings and cousins were there to say farewell. Rachel looked among her male cousins and could see the resemblance they had to Will. But she did not ask if they had ever heard from him. Her heart was too heavy with the loss of her husband. She would spend the rest of the spring in Charles Town and headed back to Brookgreen in late summer of that year.

When fall arrived it was time for the children to continue their education. Rachel had the best tutors for her children and Washington was old enough to leave home for school. He showed extraordinary talent as an artist and was lucky enough to be accepted to Harvard. Rachel was proud but also concerned. She always had Washington by her side and now he was a young man on his own. Being an artist would be a difficult profession, so Rachel made sure he was supplied with everything he needed for his journey and tuition.

Although Rachel was saddened by the thought of Washington leaving, especially after losing her husband, he thought the contrary. He looked forward to leaving the inlet and wished to see the world. And he got his wish.

Washington Allston studied not only in America but had the opportunity to sail overseas and study under some famous artistic mentors. He was away from Rachel and the plantation for many years but continued to write to his mother often. She had started to regain her life in Charles Town society and now had 2 plantations to manage. They would keep her terribly busy, but she was quite happy and proud of Washington.

Washington's style of painting caught the attention of many in the art world and he flourished. He decided to come back to America and visit friends in the New England area. While visiting a friend in Boston, Massachusetts, he met a lovely young woman. Her name was Ann Channing. She admired his work and supported his endeavors as a full-time artist.

Once the relationship became more serious in nature, Ann invited Washington to her family home for a small dinner party. When he knocked on the door to the Channing home, an older servant woman answered. Washington offered his coat and hat to the lady and asked for Miss Ann. The older woman requested his name so she could announce him. When he told her he was Washington Allston the woman froze, dropping his hat to the floor. Washington bent down, picked it up and handed it back to her. The woman offered a muttered apology and briskly left the room. As she left, Ann walked into the entryway from another direction.

"There you are, Washington. My apologies, but was not Cubby here to greet you?"

"Cubby? Is that the woman's name?" asked Washington.

"Why yes. Unusual, isn't it? She works for my father but also helps us entertain at the house. She is such a good friend. I do not know what I would do without her?"

Washington is stunned for a moment. The woman had the same name as one of the slaves that ran away when he was a toddler. He remembers his mother bringing up the matter to Washington several times over the years. Rachel had been heartbroken by the deception of Cubby's family during the time of his father's death. But after advertising Abraham's and Maryann's disappearance in the local paper, she let the matter go once she married Henry.

Washington and Ann joined the other guests and were seated at a long chestnut table for a delightful feast. The smell of oysters and pressed duck wafted from the kitchen. When the kitchen door opened, Cubby walked in with a cistern of soup. As she ladled the soup into each guest's bowl, she kept her head hung low and did not utter a word. She quickly filled the bowls and hastened back to the kitchen. Washington kept his eye on Cubby throughout the meal and noticed how she never lifted her head to join eyes with his.

At the end of the supper, Ann and Washington strolled through the courtyard outside. Washington was curious to know more about Cubby. He asked Anne where she had gotten such a name. Ann thought it was a little odd of Washington to ask about Cubby but obliged.

She explained how Cubby lost her parents when she was younger. When Cubby first came into their home, she told Ann how they worked for a kind woman but never said for whom or where they lived. Cubby told her how the family had to leave in a hurry in the night.

But unfortunately, her parents were killed. Murdered by some men, for what reason Ann did not know. Cubby never told her who the men were only that she escaped and made her way to Boston. That is when Ann's father found her. He had been an orphan himself and felt pity for Cubby. He took her in, gave her a position and she has been loyal all these years. Anne explained that Cubby could leave anytime she wished. Her father paid her quite handsomely and she was well educated. Anne added that Cubby was a painter as well, mostly flowers and such, but quite colorful and cheerful.

Washington was taken by the story Ann told. He knew what it was like to lose a parent. And Cubby had lost both her mother and father. He promptly dropped the subject and walked Ann back into the parlor and enjoyed the rest of the evening.

Washington and Ann would marry in the winter of 1809. Both traveled all across Europe and Washington studied with some of the finest painters in London and France. Ann was always at his side. Their lives were starting off beautifully and Washington would write to his mother often about their charming escapades throughout Europe.

When Rachel finally met Ann in the summer of 1810, she was accepted with open arms. Ann was a tiny little thing, with light brown curls around her face. She resembled a small China doll and Rachel immediately liked Ann. Although Rachel accepted Ann right away, she understood that Washington would be criticized for marrying a Northerner, no matter how adorable she was. Henry himself had been from Rhode Island and Rachel's family never forgave her for marrying him. Washington smiled as the two women bonded. They talked all afternoon as if they had known each other for years. He was happy to see his mother was no longer confined to just the plantation and had moved on with her life. And he never brought up the subject of Cubby.

But within the next week, Washington and Ann would have to leave for Europe and could not stay long at Brookgreen. Washington needed to get his affairs in order. His father had willed a good portion of land to him, and he needed to sell it to pay for their trip back. Rachel decided due to the intense summer heat to take them to her little cottage by the shore. The summer days were humid, and Rachel wanted to be by the water again. Washington noticed how her demeanor changed each time the family stayed on the island. She would aimlessly wander the beach for hours peering out over the waves.

The first night at the cottage was particularly windy with warm ocean breezes. The windows were all open, the curtains billowed and blew like giant sails on a voyage bound ship.

Rachel and Washington slept soundly. They were used to hearing the winds howl, but Ann had a difficult time sleeping. Her slumber was met by a terrible nightmare. She tossed and turned and nearly knocked over the oil lamp from her bedside table. She finally woke and let out a scream.

Washington was in the next bedroom and heard Ann's cry. He leapt from his bed and ran to her room. She was shaken and trembled when he took her in his arms. She began to sob and held onto Washington tightly.

Rachel heard the cries. She quickly lit a candle and walked into Ann's room. Ann wiped her tears and apologized that she disturbed the household. Rachel asked the poor girl what happened to make her scream so. Ann caught her breath and told them of her disturbing dream. At first, all she could see were ominous clouds floating all around. The sea was churning. She could hear the whistling of the winds. The rain began and she found herself on the beach. She looked toward the surf, and saw a man approach her. She described him as tall and thin, but as he got closer, she noticed he was completely covered in grey. Grey hat, grey coat, grey pants but what was most unnerving were his grey eyes. Even his eyes were grey. A grey stranger. Ann continued and said he pointed to her and said a great storm was approaching and that we must leave the island.

Ann turned toward Rachel and finished her story. "But the last thing he uttered was your name...Rachel."

Washington and Ann both looked at Rachel. Her face had gone white. White as the full moon. Her jaw dropped and a single tear fell down her cheek onto the candle flame. The light was extinguished by her tear, and they were left in total darkness while thunder clapped in the distance.

The thunder made both ladies jump and gasp. Washington rose from the bed and went to light another candle. While he was gone, Rachel gripped Ann's hand tightly.

"Tell me, did he give a name...his name?"

Ann shook her head and repeated that he only uttered Rachel's name. But she said she would never forget his eyes. They were steel grey, but they were not angry nor mad but seemed terribly sad. Although she was frightened by her grey stranger, she felt sorry for him. As if no one could hear him nor wanted to.

Rachel felt her heart break when she heard Ann recite her dream. It confirmed her greatest fear. Will was dead. She felt it when the last hurricane came to the island and destroyed every home but hers. She did not want to believe that he was gone from this world. But she believed Ann's dream. It was a warning from Will to leave the island. As she rose from the bed and started to leave the room Washington approached. He asked if Rachel wanted to be walked back to her room, but Rachel did not respond. Washington followed Rachel and watched as his mother started to pack her things. He asked why and Rachel told him that they too must pack. All of them had to leave...tonight.

"Leave, whatever for? In the middle of the night?"

"A great surge is heading for us. We must go!" exclaimed Rachel.

"But it was just a dream, mother." answered Will.

"We must go!"

Washington went back to his wife's room and told her to dress and prepare to go back to Brookgreen. Ann was just as confused as Washington.

"It was only a dream, nothing more. I must apologize for upsetting your mother."

Washington stopped Ann and again told her to dress and pack. Ann did as Washington asked and gathered their things. Rachel quickly went to the servants' quarters and woke them to prepare the carriage for the trip back. They too were confused by the request but knew not to question their mistress.

Everyone quickly entered the carriage and headed back to Brookgreen. Rachel hoped the surge would not reach the river. It also could flood if the tide rose too high. The waters could breach the riverbank into the main plantation house. As the minutes passed, the wind began to pick up. It became more difficult to maneuver the horse and carriage along the bumpy road towards the plantation. Everyone held onto each other. The ride was an unpleasant one, but they made it to Brookgreen before the storm completely unleashed.

The branches of the oak trees bowed down as if to surrender to winds. Inside the home, shutters banged and crashed against the windows. Servants rushed to close windows and board them up. Washington and Ann stayed in the parlor and waited for Rachel to join them. Rachel herself began to panic. She grabbed her bible and knelt by her bed.

"Please protect us, oh Lord. Protect my family."

Rachel then thought of one more thing. "Will, my love. Protect us all."

The rain beat down against the windows. Even the front door shook as if a giant were trying to break it down. Rachel sat with her family in the main parlor of the home. By the light of the oil lamps Rachel took out her bible and read aloud to the family. Everyone held their breath each time a tree branch fell. One branch flew through the window at the top of the staircase shattering glass down the steps. Rachel continued to read from the bible. But she also thought of Will. Was it possible that he could protect them?

Hours passed and the storm finally ended. There were broken windows and many pine and oak tree branches covered the landscape. Later that day after clearing debris at Brookgreen, Washington along with a few servants went back to attend to the damage to the cottage. They found the cottage secure. There was only one difference at the property. It looked like a small wall had been built around it made of pluff mud, reeds, and sand. It looked like a dam were constructed to hold back the ocean tide that flowed straight over the island. It diverted the water to one side, saving the small building from being washed away in the current.

Washington had never seen anything like this before. He could only assume that Rachel was right about Ann's dream. It was a prophetic message...but from whom?

Unfortunately, others in the area were not so lucky. News came from Pawleys, Murrells Inlet and Charles Town that some had not fared so well. There was flooding throughout Rachel's sibling's plantation homes. Her aunt and uncle's home suffered water damage too. Most of Charles Town did. This was a price that was often paid for living on the coast of Carolina. It would take days and weeks for the communities to recover. But Rachel knew how lucky they were compared to others. She knew she had a guardian angel with her. Her only question was why Will appeared to Ann and not to her. Why?

Within a few days, Washington and Ann left for London. Rachel helped her son sell the land his father willed him and went with them to the port in Georgetown to say farewell. They stood together on the dock in the early morning mist. Rachel hugged Ann and her son goodbye and waved as they boarded the ship. It was time to return to her home and to the duties of managing the plantations.

Chapter Nine

Washington and Ann traveled throughout Europe from 1810 until 1815 while his career blossomed. They had just rented their first home and were creating the perfect married life for themselves in London. Rachel received letters from her son quite often and was so proud of his success. The last letter she received regarded Washington's health. He had suffered from pain in his torso area but had recovered due to the constant devotion of his wife Ann. Rachel was afraid her son may be ill again. She had not heard from him in weeks and waited anxiously for a note from him. In time, a letter from London addressed to Rachel finally arrived.

It was devastating news from Washington. His young wife, Ann, only 36 years of age had taken ill and died within days. There was no known cause for her death. It was as if the angel of death had decided to take her without a long, drawn-out illness. She just simply felt ill one day and passed. Rachel could tell from Washington's letter that he suffered greatly from the loss of Ann. The funeral had been a small affair and his heart ached to the point where he could not work. He was also saddened by the fact they never had children and he felt completely alone. Although he had many good friends in London, he found he was homesick for America and would come back in the near future once he had energy to do so.

Rachel wept when she read his letter. How she wished she were there with him to ease his broken heart. She was, however, glad to hear that he would be back to see her again. Rachel had lost many of her family and friends over the years and she was unsure of her own destiny. How long would she have?

In time, Washington returned to America and would visit his mother and siblings at Brookgreen. But his heart was heavy, and he did not seem the same. His paintings would reveal themes of death and angels. He had stopped writing poetry. Rachel hoped that being back along the inlet would help him through his bereavement period. It always gave her a sense of calm. Her thoughts were clearer when she walked on the sandy beach. She hoped the salt air would help Washington with his grief and it did. He picked up his paintbrush and started creating portraits once more. He even created a beautiful portrait of his mother, which Rachel would cherish to her dying day.

Rachel was glad that Washington started creating works of art again and eventually he travelled back to England. She was quite proud of all her children. They had all grown up and created their own lives. She watched her one son Henry enter politics and become mayor and the others marry and raise children. Life was sweet. At least for a while. Because there was always that one thing that no one in the family could control...mother nature.

It was September 27, 1822.

Rachel had spent the last week at her cottage home on the island. This was the first time she was completely alone in the house. She decided to go without a servant or any of her children or grandchildren. She felt she needed to be alone in her thoughts. She just passed a milestone. She turned 65 years old and outlived most of her family members. She had decided after the death of Henry to never marry again. She did not wish to go through the heartbreak of losing another husband.

And she still thought of Will. After all these years she still thought of her first love and how life could have been. She remembered how young they were. How unsure she was. She felt guilty that she had not mustered the courage to start a life with Will. It would not be until she met Henry that she became the strong woman she was now. Her life had been full, but she could not understand why she continued to think of Will. He had died so many years before. But it was as though she could feel his presence around her whenever she returned to the island.

As Rachel walked back from the dunes to her cottage, she noticed the winds had begun to change direction from the southeast. This made her stop and take notice of the sky. There were clouds over the horizon, dark grey ones. She assumed a thunderstorm was brewing and turned back toward the house. But something stopped her. A chill ran down her spine. She shook it off and took another step. But she stopped again. She turned toward the churning ocean and watched a mist develop before her eyes. She thought it was fog but that seemed unlikely this time of day. But this fog did not roll onto the beach. It began to take shape. It grew taller as it approached Rachel. She took a step back but could not keep her eyes off the mist. It became darker in color and more solid in form. She blinked her eyes tightly and opened repeatedly but the form continued to grow. The outline of a man molded out of the mist. He continued to form arms and legs and the outline of a coat and hat appeared. The face was the last to emerge. A grey beard, moustache and finally his eyes. His steel grey eyes.

Rachel was terrified and frozen in her tracks. She could not move. Was she actually seeing this? Was this real? She found the courage to take a step toward the grey stranger. Then another. Then she locked eyes with the grey man.

"Will!" Rachel cried out his name and started to run towards the figure, her arms open. Before she was able to hold him in her arms, the figure lifted his right hand. She stopped suddenly. She was only 10 feet from him. She took another step, and the grey man held his hand up again.

"Do not approach. There is no time. Please heed my warning. A dangerous storm is approaching. Please leave the island now!"

"Will, it is you! Do you not know me? It is your Rachel."

The grey man gently smiled. Rachel tried once more to approach Will, but he held his hand up again.

"Please, dearest Rachel, you must go now!"

Rachel noticed Will's hand slowly faded in front of her. His arm was next. He turned away and started back towards the ocean. With each step he faded more and more until there was nothing left but footprints in the sand.

"Will... Will, do not leave me. Do not go!" cried Rachel. By the time she finished her sentence, Will had completely disappeared into the foamy sea.

Rachel fell to her knees, dropped her head into her hands and wept. The wind whipped sand all around her like a small cyclone. It was then she heard a voice wafting all around her.

"I shall love you forever, my Rachel. I am forever yours."

Rachel held her head up and wiped her tears. Will was nowhere to be seen but she could hear his voice softly repeating the words. She pulled herself up and swiftly ran back to her cottage. Quickly packing her things, she stopped for a moment and looked around the house. She wondered if her home would still be standing after the surge. She remembered each time a storm occurred on the island, her tiny home was spared. Would it be spared again?

Rachel threw her belongings into the carriage and hitched her horse. The wind continued to gust, and her horse became skittish. Rachel grabbed the reins tighter and took control of the animal while she prayed for a safe return to Brookgreen. The path back was a difficult one, the road was uneven, and the carriage could not go any faster. It rocked back and forth. Twice the buggy nearly toppled over but she regained her balance and continued. After a treacherous ride, Rachel made it back to the plantation.

The servants and slaves had closed the windows and shutters. Animals were taken to higher pastures. Everyone felt the danger coming. Even the snakes had left their underground refuge and headed to higher ground. The communities and towns tried to prepare in what little time there was. They prayed that their homes and their lives would be spared. But not everyone would be.

The storm landed late afternoon between Charles Town and Pawleys Island. It was a massive surge with winds as much as 100 miles per hour. But the worst of the storm was not the wind but the surf. It came when the tide had just begun to rise. The gale force winds, and blinding rain continued throughout the night. There were slaves that lived in the area called Santee; a particular region of the low country south of Brookgreen. There was no high ground on their plantations. They could not run to seek higher ground on another property, or they would be considered runaways. Many were forced to climb to the roof of their shanties. Others climbed trees and held on for dear life. But the surge swept in higher and higher. It carried their small dwellings away as if they were made of twigs. The river continued to rise and swallowed everything and everyone in its path. Horses tried desperately to swim through the rough currents. Cattle could not reach high ground and were pulled under the water. Entire families were clinging to the mighty oak trees. Cries of children were heard as they were ripped away from their parent's arms. In desperation, parents dove into the waves in the hope of rescuing their babies. But no one resurfaced. Torrential rain fell throughout the night. It was more than had been seen in years. Copious amounts of rain fell in torrents and the rivers rose to their highest levels. And the cries continued through the darkness.

Then...silence. The eye of the storm had drifted over just after midnight. People caught their breath briefly and began to call out to family in the dark. They did not have much time. The eye would pass quickly, and the worst of the storm was on its way. Everyone knew the worst was still yet to come.

The Waccamaw river near Brookgreen was swollen and rose upward towards the main house. Rachel saw her slaves head to the stone smokehouse building near the back of her home. It was built specifically with a small tower for slaves to use in case of flooding. She called out to them to seek shelter in her home, but her voice could not be heard through the intense noise of the storm. She herself was at its mercy. She could do nothing more than pray. She reached for her bible and read aloud.

"Yea, though I walk through the valley of the shadow of death, I shall fear no evil, for you are with me; your rod and your staff, they comfort me."

Rachel repeated the verse over and over again. Each time reciting it louder and louder as the wind and rain came back to claim the land. The trunks that were created to be small dams along the river were breached and the Waccamaw overflowed its banks. The rice fields were demolished, corn washed away, trees were uprooted, and all living creatures were left in the cold quagmire of mud and pitch darkness. Mother nature took control of this night. And she would not release her fury until the early morning light.

When morning came, and the sun brought light to the plantation there was only the horror of death. Rachel could only stare out the door of her home to find her gardens and fields washed away. The water had risen as high as the top step of her home, but luckily did not enter. Unfortunately, her fireplace chimney had fallen during the night and water had flowed in from the roof. She had been spared and went in search of her servants. She walked out onto her porch and yelled for them by name. She was too frightened to go to the smokehouse to witness the trauma that might be behind the door. As the old wooden door creaked open, her servants walked out. All were exhausted, soaked to the bone, and crying. The waters had reached knee high inside the smokehouse but otherwise, they were all accounted for.

Rachel fell to her knees, her bible still in her hand. Her slaves raised their hands to the clear blue sky and called out to the Lord and thanked Him repeatedly. All of them knew a miracle had just occurred.

It took weeks for Murrells Inlet to have debris and fields cleaned. It would be too late to plant rice so any morsel of grain, sweet potato or ear of corn had to be salvaged otherwise all would go hungry. Livestock had been washed away and the alligators would feast on their carcasses. But not only were beasts washed away, but humans as well. For weeks, families traveled all around the county to look for loved ones. Once the newspaper in Georgetown started printing again, the news became grimmer with each edition. By last count, nearly 300 people had died. Most were slaves of the Santee region. They had no place to run and huddled in their tiny shacks. On North Island alone, approximately 125 slaves were washed away along with a respected doctor and his family of 15; men, women, and children. Many others were missing throughout Georgetown and Murrells Inlet. Most of Charles Town had also received damage from large trees that toppled on buildings, stables, and carriage houses.

Over the following weeks, bloated bodies would be found beneath the marsh reeds along the inlet and mangled rice plants along the river. The stench of decay could be smelled for miles. Mosquitoes and flies became unbearable, and disease would overwhelm every household.

Yellow fever, malaria, and cholera swept over the county. Slaves would die from malnutrition brought on by their poor diets or lack of food. What food was left was unhealthy. The death count increased due to disease and starvation. Only those families who had learned lessons from mother nature in the past kept storehouses of food in case of shortages. Rachel was one of those people. She had meat and fish kept in salt barrels but that would only last for so long. Barrels of grain were kept up high in the barns and would aid in feeding the locals but only if sea water had not contaminated it.

Soon, repairs had to be made on the main house and slave shanties were rebuilt. Fields were cleared and livestock that had run off the land were sought and brought back. Many would simply feed on fresh fish and oysters. That would be their salvation. But disease would be their enemy.

Rachel found many of her servants had become ill. Malaria was widespread and doctors could do very little for the sick. Due to sickness and the time of year, planting would have to wait.

After some grueling months, once the main property was repaired and she had a moment to herself, Rachel went back to Pawleys Island. She was anxious about what horrors she would encounter. She rode her horse down the path through the dunes and held her hand above her eyes to shade them from the sun. As she got closer, a smile appeared on her face. Besides a few palmetto trees that had fallen from the storm, her house was still there. Her tiny bungalow was unharmed. She was dumbfounded. The trees that had fallen just missed the home by inches. Although water had climbed over the island during the storm, the trees worked together as a channel.

Rachel eyes filled with tears. She sat upon the front step of her cottage and thanked God...and Will. He was her guardian angel disguised as a grey man.

Over the course of her life, Rachel felt Will's presence each time the weather became dangerous. Her health and her age would keep her from returning to Pawleys Island whenever she wanted. Her children would help her run the plantations, but they insisted she stay in Charles Town close to family. When she turned 70 years old she decided it would be best to go back to her home in Charles Town. She no longer had the strength to go to Pawleys Island unless she had help.

It was Christmas of 1839 and Rachel was surrounded by family at her home. By midday she was exhausted by the merriment of the holiday. She kissed her grandchildren and excused herself. She told her children she just needed a moment or two to lie down and to wake her when dinner was announced. Her son, Henry offered to walk her to her room. She took him by his arm, and they walked the long hall together. He reached to open her chamber door. Rachel turned and smiled.

"My child, I do believe I can accomplish the rest of the way."

Henry laughed and gave his mother a small bow. Rachel entered her bedroom and closed the door behind her. As soon as she laid upon the bed, she felt she was not alone. She looked around the room but saw nothing unusual. Once she laid back down, she felt a tightness within her chest. She thought she was only tired, and she fell into a deep sleep.

Rachel found herself on the beach on Pawleys Island. As she walked along the sandy shore, the wind picked up and the surf flooded towards her. She was swept up by the waves and began to drift under the current. But she felt no fear or pain. Only the warmth of the ocean tide. Suddenly, a light appeared. A beautiful, radiant light pulsating like the sun above her head. Then, she saw a hand reach down towards her from out of the light. She recognized this hand. It was a grey hand. She reached upwards and touched the end of the fingers. Their hands clasped together tightly. The hand gently pulled her up out of the water and towards the light. There was a sudden rush of warmth as she felt herself and her grey man lifted upwards towards the magnificent illumination. Rachel would never let go of his hand ever again.

Today my neighbors on the South Strand and Waccamaw Neck area still keep vigil for the Grey Man when the winds begin to blow, and the ocean seas rise. We live in an age of modern radar and television weather reporters that give us warnings of impending hurricanes. We have days to prepare for the event instead of just minutes. But we in the Pawleys Island area still look for the Grey Man. If you are lucky enough to see him wandering on the sandy beach before a great storm then you, your family and your property will be spared. But heed his warning. If you do see him, run! Because his job is to save your life.

About the Author

Christine Vernon was born and raised in Plymouth Meeting, PA. She was trained in oil and acrylic painting and continues to sell her artwork at her home studio. She moved to South Carolina in 2005 to a small fishing village named Murrells Inlet where she became the local storyteller and lecturer for different venues. Christine created a local ghost and history tour where she regales her guests of the legends, history and ghost stories of the South Strand.

Read more at www.miss-chris-inlet-walking-tour.business.site.